12 —
CAN LIT
12/19

Carol **Bruneau**

George Elliott **Clarke**

Christy Ann **Conlin**

Kelly **Cooper**

Libby **Creelman**

Michael **Crummey**

Larry **Lynch**

Rabindranath **Maharaj**

Lisa **Moore**

Peter **Norman**

Karen **Smythe**

Lee D. **Thompson**

R.M. **Vaughan**

Michael **Winter**

VICTORY MEAT

New Fiction FROM Atlantic Canada

Edited by Lynn Coady

ANCHOR CANADA

Anchor Canada and colophon are trademarks.

NATIONAL LIBRARY OF CANADA CATALOGUING IN PUBLICATION

Victory meat : new fiction from Atlantic Canada / Lynn Coady, editor.

ISBN 0-385-65892-3

1. Short stories, Canadian (English)—Maritime Provinces. 2. Canadian fiction
(English)—21st century. I. Coady, Lynn, 1970–

PS8329.5.M37V43 2003   C813'.01089715   C2002-905446-X
PR9197.32.V43 2003

Cover image (sign): Lynne Reeder
Printed and bound in Canada

Published in Canada by Anchor Canada,
a division of Random House of Canada Limited

Visit Random House of Canada Limited's website:
www.randomhouse.ca

TRANS   10   9   8   7   6   5   4   3   2   1

CONTENTS

INTRODUCTION

Books that say Arse

THE PROBLEM IS, WHENEVER A DISTINCTIVE CULTURE, like that of Atlantic Canada, is taken note of by a larger culture, like Canada, two things happen simultaneously. On the one hand, the distinctive culture gets marginalized: Newfoundlander jokes, disparagement by Upper Canadian politicians. The second is an offshoot of the first, but is much wider-ranging, seemingly benign, and therefore insidious: the culture gets fetishized. I can offer many more examples of this than I can of straightforward marginalization, but it doesn't make me feel any better about things. You've got your *Road to Avonlea,* your "traditional" music (these days just as bland and overproduced as anything you'd hear on a Top 40 radio station), an expectation of "simplicity" which is actually more often than not an expectation of poverty and ignorance. Stereotypes, no matter how well intentioned, are ultimately never compliments. The experience is of some oblivious yahoo four-wheeling his Bronco across the complex bionetwork of your very identity. "What a cute little town!" (Actually, this was once my universe.) "I love these wooden lobster traps!" (But nobody uses that kind anymore — they're built specifically for you to purchase and take home.) "Look at these gorgeous old houses!" (They have been bought and restored by Germans — or Americans, or the Swiss — because no one from here can afford them anymore.) "Look at these quaint little houses!" (With their satellite dishes on the lawns.)

Yet this experience of fetishization is a tango, a dance that requires two. Note the enthusiasm in the expressions above, note the adjectives ("gorgeous!") and the verbs ("love!"). It's the hyperbole of romantic infatuation, and how can the object of infatuation not respond? We see ourselves anew in the lover's eyes: Gee, I always thought Great Uncle Bob's place was a shitbox, but apparently it's been "quaint" all this time. My grandparents' music — the stuff that used to grate on my teenage ears — is suddenly "haunting," just like the landscape that was, for so many years, simply the place where I lived. It's like being told your hair is like silk and your eyes are limpid pools. Swoon. You fall in love right back — you give the lover what he wants. He comes home one night holding out a kilt? By God, you put it on and dance him a Highland fling for good measure. And so the tourism industry of eastern Canada was born.

But you can't do that with art. ("Sure you can," was the Nova Scotia government's pronouncement recently, stamping out the province's independent Arts Council and Frankensteining it back to life under the rubric of "Tourism and Culture.") Okay, then, let me amend that. You can *try* to do that with art — as lots of people have. The results have been unfortunate. To push the metaphor about as far as it will go, after a while the kilt starts to chafe. You start to feel silly. *This isn't me.* You'd like to be able to just hang out in your housecoat every now and again like a regular person.

What I'm describing is a maturation process, I suppose; every initial infatuation must inevitably mature into respect or else degrade into contempt — the contempt I have described above. It can also be called resentment, the other side of infatuation, when instead of fetishizing a culture that clearly differs from the one you inhabit, you become annoyed with it. You make fun of the accent, so to speak, as if it's not genuine, but some kind of folksy contrivance affected to score personality points. Somebody told me recently of a complaint some writer made about "all these new books from the east coast that say 'arse.'" So resentment — the state of the disenchanted lover — permeates the arts community too, but to me it's like complaining about British novels for using words like "chap" and calling elevators "lifts." Yes, we say "arse." We also use email, collect Air Miles, and have the entire third season of *Buffy the Vampire Slayer* on DVD.

Which is to say, Atlantic Canadians, and Atlantic Canadian writers, have grown up right alongside of the rest of the Western world. It might have taken some of us a bit longer to shed our mullets (I'm not quite sure for what I'm using the mullet as a metaphor in this instance — perhaps it's not a metaphor at all), but the point is, we exist in the here and now, no matter how unfashionable our hairdos. Bemoan it if you will, the way of the world, how the cultural fault lines have merged, solidified, in the past century. I choose to look at the bright side: we have matured. In time, we all of us have cut off our rat-tails. The new literary work coming from the Atlantic provinces very much demands your respect, as you will see. You will enjoy it no matter where in the world you are — not for reasons of nostalgia or quaintness but because it's just so good.

A word on Victory Meat

It happened like this: in Fredericton, New Brunswick, in 1994, I opened up *The Fiddlehead* and read a story called "Bitches on All Sides" by Rabindranath Maharaj. The story was set in Fredericton, the city where I was living at the time. Everything about it was *right* — absolutely right, I thought. Meaning that everything about it seemed true and familiar to me. Later, though, I realized that what I actually liked about the story was that nothing about it was familiar at all. To break it down: "Bitches on All Sides" is the story of alienation in Atlantic Canada. It is about being alone, isolated, and utterly outside of the world you at once inhabit. My point is: everything I knew about "Maritime" literature had equipped me to expect the opposite. Atlantic Canadian writing was supposed to be about *home,* about belonging — extended families, close-knit communities, and a shared cultural language and identity. "Bitches" had nothing to do with any of this. My revelation lay in the fact that I identified with it as a reader more strongly than anything I had read that accorded to the eastern Canadian formula described above. At-Can myths and stereotypes started keeling over in my mind like dominoes from that moment on. Perhaps our writing could be just as true, vivid, and familiar without following the over-trod paths hacked out for us in days gone by — paths that served their purpose at one time, but have since been made redundant by the advent of planes, trains and automobiles — not to mention lots of other less-tried paths. It still gives me a thrill to discover the iconoclastic core in the work of writers like R.M. Vaughan with his horrific twist on the quintessential Maritime "homecoming" story, or Lisa Moore's Newfoundland road trip, driving the reader right up to the door of a less media-friendly aspect of eastern Canada—parochial and moralizing.

Finally, about Fredericton: Fredericton is weird. It has a museum that houses, for some reason, a giant fibreglass frog. It has a place called the Victory Meat Market, which has a neon sign that looks as if it's from another era — not the era that defines downtown Fredericton's overall aesthetic, which is quaint, turn-of-the-century Atlantic Canadian gothic (meaning not too gothic but gothic enough to be picturesque). The Victory Meat Market is of a more recent vintage, with an impertinent, gritty sort of toughness that has yet to be buffed over by the well-meaning architects of nostalgia and sentiment who have always wielded such power in the Atlantic provinces. Victory Meat takes no shit. It's there to sell meat, damnit, not postcards, miniature province-of-New-Brunswick beer mugs, designer jams, or hooked rugs. At the same time there's a post-war, can-do sort of pugnacity about the place. We're gonna sell the hell out of this meat and who's to say otherwise?

The Victory Meat Market is both out of, and in keeping with, the character of Fredericton — and, by extension, the Atlantic provinces — all at once. Which in some ways makes it typical — if that makes any sense.

Lynn Coady

BITCHES ON ALL SIDES

Rabindranath Maharaj

ONE DAY, EXACTLY A MONTH AFTER HIS ARRIVAL in Fredericton, Ramjohn sat on a concrete bench in the Regent Mall and reviewed his life. His forty-two years in Caura were ordered with a thin glamour, which he knew to be false and which left him with an indeterminate tiredness levelling out into despair. Caura was too far and his enemies too removed, the distance putting them beyond his reach and dislodging their utility. He concentrated instead on his more immediate irritants. Shoppers breezed by, clutching substantial bags in their pink, plump hands. Children engrossed in a video game squirmed and contorted as they fingered knobs and buttons. A young couple on a nearby bench caressed each other, oblivious to the dishevelled prosperity swirling around.

Ramjohn widened his focus and looked for signs of suffering, some random misfortune to soothe his anxiety. He felt a moderate satisfaction in the observation that most of the men were bald or balding, but this brief joy was diminished by the intrusive thought of his own thinning hair. He felt defeated, isolated, persecuted. Someone sat on the bench next to him. He did not look around but guessed that it was an old woman so afflicted by senility or by cataracts that she could not detect their difference in colour.

"So where you from, man, India or Pakistan?"

"From the West Indies," Ramjohn said, taking a deep breath.

"The West Indies? *Rasclat,* man. What part?" Ramjohn saw the plump, smiling Jamaican, his dreadlocks contained within a huge purple cap.

"Caura," he said, undecided about whether he appreciated this intrusion. But the Jamaican was friendly and he spoke with an easy familiarity.

"How the rass you land up in this place, man? You staying with relatives?"

"No," Ramjohn said, biting his lips. Against his will, he felt himself responding to the proffered friendliness, to the West Indian accent. "I renting from one of these big-shot landlord."

The Jamaican whistled. "Them man is parasite, man. But how you end up here insteada Toronto or someway in Ontario?"

Ramjohn passed his hand over his hair and explained how he had seen brochures on Maine, verdant and idyllic-looking, and since it was easier to get a Canadian visa than an American, he had chosen the nearest Canadian province.

The Jamaican laughed loudly, attracting the attention of a few shoppers. "But you is a real *bambaclat,* man. You know how far Maine is from here?"

"Yes," Ramjohn said in a sad voice. "I discover that when I already reach. But it look so close in the atlas."

"Choosing out a place from a brochure," the Jamaican said. "That is craziness of the highest order. But why you wanted to come across here — or in Maine — for?"

Dreams bolstered by desperation. He thought: I am in a little cottage in the midst of a forest of fir and pine, churning out essays for *Newsweek* and *Time* and *The New Yorker*. In the evenings I sally down to the little brook and scoop out slick salmon, and at nights I work on my novel. Sometimes while I am walking in the forest or while I am fishing, wondrous poems sprinkle into my mind and I rush to my little cottage to record lines which will never be published but will instead be placed in an iron chest and passed on from generation to generation. I am apart now from those who spurned my talent and laughed at my treatises on the nature of existence. Those from my own island who mocked my noble mission and my genius. Now I am beyond these Philistines forever.

Such dreams are sullied neither by matters such as rent and food nor by daily frustrations.

"Look, man, haul you ass and leave me alone, you hear? All you West Indian like real parasite, appearing all over the damn place." Ramjohn got up and walked away sulkily. The couple on the nearby bench stared at the fat, black man with the huge cap and gaping mouth.

About one week later, while Ramjohn was seated on the same bench, he saw her. He was searching, as usual, for signs of discomfort among the shoppers, while keeping a wary eye for the Jamaican. She was thin, plain, and wearing a sweater several sizes too big. But he was drawn by the furtive expression on her face and by an evasiveness he found beguiling. She saw him staring at her and went quickly into a clothing store, but Ramjohn noticed that while she pretended to appraise some item of clothing she continuously flicked furtive little glances at him.

When the sales clerk came up to her, Ramjohn saw the embarrassment on her small, plain face. He waited, wondering what he should do. If he were a smoker, he would have lit a cigarette and nonchalantly puffed rings into the air while he pondered his next move. He saw a discarded flyer on the bench and grabbed it and pretended to read. When he looked up she was no longer in the store, but then he noted with some uneasiness that she was walking straight toward him. She sat on the bench.

"Any bargains?"

"What?" Then he remembered the flyer in his hands. "No. Nothing to suit my taste." For the next five minutes they remained silent. Then he asked her, "You living here in Fredericton?" He saw her furtiveness re-emerging and added quickly, "I renting down on York Street, but the lease up in the next few days."

In the next half-hour, everything was arranged. When his lease expired, Ramjohn would move in with her and they would share the rent and other expenses. It was purely a business arrangement and there was no promise of intimacy on either side. Like Ramjohn, she had depleted her meagre savings, and this pooling of resources would make life easier for both of them.

In the days that followed, Ramjohn managed — in spite of her reticence — to piece together the fragments of her story. Originally from Guyana, she was quite likely an illegal immigrant who had moved from Toronto to Fredericton to reduce the chances of being caught. But while Fredericton, because of its distance from Toronto, temporarily offered a safe haven, it offered little else. There was no work, and both food and rent were expensive. Several times she had considered moving back to

Toronto and taking her chances there, but as news reached her about other Guyanese who had been caught and deported she decided to remain and hope that things would improve. Ramjohn learned other surprising things. She told him about the Salvation Army store, where he could purchase used clothing for next to nothing. And about the food bank, where he could, once a month, collect groceries donated by bakeries or food stores that could not otherwise get rid of them. For a while his anger was replaced by a less enervating guilt.

Each night, while sleeping on the boxspring in the living room, he would feel a vague satisfaction in having met her. And every night he would hear the couple in the adjoining apartment thumping and groaning. He tried to imagine them, attempted to visualize their coupling, but it was useless. He stood outside his door during the early mornings and evenings, but he saw neither entry nor departure. Perhaps they never left their apartment. Yet he was able to synchronize all their nightly activities. The few preliminary creaks of the bed, then the frenzied rocking, and finally the groaning and pleading. Timing them, he would rush to the toilet to catch some bit of revelatory conversation, but all he would hear were their faint footsteps and the flushing of the toilet. He discovered that, by placing his ear over the electrical outlet on the wall next to his boxspring, he could hear pieces of conversation.

In the meantime, she read old magazines she had borrowed from the library and wrote letters. He often wondered about her letter writing, but whenever he passed by the table she would quickly cover the letter with a magazine and pretend she was reading some article. He found himself becoming irritated by her plain, almost lifeless features and by her casual evasiveness. Gradually she became a part of his larger anxiety; because she could not share his misery, she must somehow be responsible for it. One night while his ear was affixed to the outlet she passed by to go to the kitchen. He saw her staring at him and he removed his ear from against the wall. Anger suffused his thin, long frame.

"What the ass you looking at?" he shouted. "You never see anybody eavesdropping before?" His head dropped on the pillows. "It have anything else to do in this place?"

Later that night he decided against any further eavesdropping in that manner since he was suddenly struck by the idea that the couple in the adjoining apartment might discover this invasion of their privacy and decide to push some sharp, pointed object into the outlet and straight into his ear. He grimaced with an imagined pain. That night he went to sleep festering in impotent anger.

The next morning at the breakfast table he told her, "I going to look for a job today." She continued to apply butter to her bread. Two hours later he returned, slamming the door and flinging his sweater on the table. She came from the kitchen and waited, wiping her hands on a tea towel. Ramjohn tore off his shirt and threw it on the television. She heard him grinding his teeth.

"Any luck?" she asked.

"Luck?" He looked up at the ceiling. "Luck, you say? Okay, let me see. It have lock-up, lock-neck, lock-jaw, loch-ness, what kind you really talking about? Ohhh, is bad-luck you mean. Why you didn't say so all the time?" He looked down; it was difficult to maintain this sarcasm in the face of his steadily increasing anger. "Yes, Miss Illegal Immigrant, I had plenty of that." The pain in her face reinforced his anger. "Don't watch me so because that is how all of them does see we as. Illegal immigrant! Alien! Leech! Parasite from a next country coming to sponge off them." He sat on the sofa, almost missing the edge. "And when I think how all them newspapers in Caura use to be chasing me down to write this and write that." He felt comforted by the lie. "The best blasted journalist — no, *columnist* in the whole island — and over here I not even good to wash pot or clean floor. And you know what does really eat me up? How they so blasted polite with everything. 'Sorry, sir, we have nothing now. Maybe you can try again next month.' As if next month they will suddenly start liking black people."

During the next few weeks, he left every morning and returned within two hours, flinging various items of clothing on the furniture. And she soon realized that his rage was not discriminatory but embraced all ethnic groups, every nationality. Once, after having been spurned by the owner of a Chinese restaurant, he told her, "These Chinese and them is the worst race on the face of the earth. You ever watch them carefully and see how the top part of them so well proportion and muscular and from the waist down how they thin and dry-up? Like if a big polio epidemic pass over the whole of Hong Kong before they come here."

Another day he told her, "In me whole life I never bounce up bitches like them Indian and them. Not the West Indian species, eh, but the kind from India. They come from a place where the people don't think nothing about shitting all over the road and in the train station cool-cool, and over here they does act as if they still in they blasted back yard. I don't know why the Canadian government don't deport all they tail to Calcutta straightaway. If I was the prime minister I woulda ship them back first kissmeass thing in the morning. And the part I does can't understand is the way they does look down on we Indian from the West Indies, as if we is some lower quality model. Just imagine, this half-dead little bitch who running a stall in the Farmer's Market have the guts to say that he can't help me because when he come here, nobody help *he* out. One setta conniving, money-hungry nastiness if you ask me."

Each morning she calculated the amount of money spent on food and rent and the amount remaining, and each day Ramjohn's anger became more expansive. Once he told her, "The worst variety of Canadians is the people who came from Poland and places in that direction. Wherever they go, they does cause trouble. They creating one packa confusion in Europe, and over here, if you just give them the chance, they will start with the same nonsense in no time. I don't know why Hitler didn't finish off all of them before they had a chance to come up here. Racist and hoodlum."

Standing at the kitchen table, she asked him in a patient voice, "But Ramjohn, I thought you say that it's the German people who are criminals?"

"I look like a blasted historian to you?" he hissed. "Ain't you fully well know what I mean?" He searched for a connection. After a while he said, "All of them is Nazis. That is me point." He turned his face away and in spite of his rage he smiled, his narrow cheeks fleshing out, comforting his long nose.

But such moments of satisfaction were brief. He stopped looking for jobs, and each morning he would wander in and out of stores and government buildings. He often paused and stared at workers. They responded with uneasy looks and frowns. Once, while peering through a glass door at a young woman working on a computer, he pulled down his eyelids with his index fingers and his lower lip with his thumbs. Then he flattened his face against the glass. The young woman looked up and screamed. Ramjohn walked on.

Slowly, the notion that the whole of Fredericton was involved in some kind of conspiracy against him took hold. He was certain that the postal worker had placed her thumb on the scale when she was weighing a parcel he was sending to Caura. Another extra gram for me to pay for, he thought. I wonder what she woulda do if I did grab she damn thumb and wring it out. Once when he was rushing out of a supermarket he bounced his head on the automatic door which was just beginning to open. He kicked the door savagely and hobbled away. In the apartment he would sit morosely in front of the television, then spring up and shout, "Bitches! Bitches on all side!" It became his favourite expression.

Sometimes she would come and sit on a chair some distance away and stare remotely at the curtainless window while Ramjohn simmered in rage. Then one day she told him, "I'm going to look for a job."

"What?"

"I'm going to try to find a job. We don't have much money left."

"Okay, go ahead. It have hundreds of jobs just waiting for illegal immigrants in this place. All you have to do is just go and inform them that you illegal and they will find a job for you in no time."

She remained silent for a while, then said, "We only have enough money for about three months. We wouldn't be able to afford this apartment after that."

"Apartment? You call this an apartment? Forty-two Tweedledum Street. Tweedledum! Run outside quick and see if it have seven dwarf living in the next apartment, or check and see if is Rapunzel or Humpty Dumpty peeping out from the next building. I don't know what kinda madman will give a street a name like that. You know how shame I does be to put Tweedledum as the return address on any letter I write?" When he turned around, she was gone. "Bitches. Bitches on all side," he muttered.

When she returned, Ramjohn was still in front of the television. He pretended he was examining his toenails. "So what happen?" he enquired in a tone of deliberate calmness. "They make you manager of McDonald's?" She placed a bag in the kitchen and went to her room. Ramjohn squeezed and tugged at a toenail. After about five minutes he shouted, "Is okay, you know. You could tell me, I wouldn't report you." She came and sat on the chair. "This damn toenail," Ramjohn screamed, unable to curtain his impatience. "Bitches!"

"I get a job."

The foot, suddenly disengaged, fell heavily on the floor. "What sorta job?" he asked.

"As a babysitter. I really went to McDonald's, but in the application form they gave me I am supposed to provide a social insurance number and names of referees."

"Just like a soccer match, eh?" he said awkwardly.

"Anyway," she continued, "while I was seated by the table reading the form, a woman came to me and we started to talk. She is working at the university and she wants a babysitter on weekdays."

"She know your status?" he asked.

"I suppose so. I didn't tell her, though."

"Babysitting, eh? What you know about baby? This is not black people baby we talking about here, you know. One knock in the head for crying, two knock for messing, and four-five good solid knock when they playing sick."

"In Guyana I had eight younger brothers and sisters," she said in a soft voice. "My mother died when I was twelve years."

And for the first time Ramjohn could find nothing appropriate to say.

She left every morning at eight and returned at four. Ramjohn, hearing the door's click, would rush to the sofa and switch on the television. He would cast quick, furtive glances at her and wait for some information about her job. But she offered nothing, and later during the night he would fall asleep hearing the squealing and moaning in the adjoining apartment. She bought new clothes for herself and, once, denim trousers for him. He put on the trousers over the faded cotton ones he was wearing. "Ooh, like I come a young boy again." He spun around. "But you don't find that it making my bottom look long and flat?" She smiled. And Ramjohn, looking at her, suddenly realized that the furtive expression was gone. That night he cursed himself for this expression of weakness. Lying on the bed, he realized that the barrier of anger that had strengthened him for so long was now thinning away into an impotent petulance, diminishing into a weak, despairing joke. He fell asleep and dreamed that he was holding a piece of his penis in his hand. He had no idea of how it broke off, how he ended up holding it in his hand, but he saw that it was spongy, like a piece of gizzard. He tried to stick it on, but the parts did not match — the broken piece, gorged with blood, thicker, and the injured member thin and wispy.

When Ramjohn awoke he knew that he had to act. He considered jumping from the top of the museum with a banner stating, "For those who didn't have the courage." But then he thought: Why should I suffer? Why should I die? His mind moved in other directions. Vague thoughts of terrorist activities filtered into his mind and faded just as quickly. He felt claustrophobic. Pushing off the blanket, he rushed outside. And then, for the first time, he saw the couple from the adjoining apartment. They seemed to be leaving for some trip, and Ramjohn stared at the fat woman tugging an overfilled suitcase and the man, some distance behind, old, stooped and dirty-looking, staring at the ground, dragging his feet. And at that moment two things happened. Ramjohn's anger returned, and he knew exactly what he had to do.

Inside Victory Meat Market, he sustained his rage by thinking of the pig as a fat, dirty, stupid, ungainly animal. He grabbed the chunk of meat from the freezer, sniffed it in a professional manner, then slammed it roughly into his trolley, startling the cashier, a fat, freckled, young woman who had been staring at him with trepidation. He wheeled the trolley recklessly towards her, pulled out the meat from the trolley and banged it on the counter. She jumped. He pushed his face close to her and asked, "How much for this . . . this meat?"

"Six-fifty," she said, her fingers nervously clutching the sides of her cash register. "The price is on the package. Six-fifty."

He threw back his head and laughed. "Six-fifty for a fat, nasty piece of pig!"

"Yes, sir," she said tentatively, glancing toward the manager's office. "Will that be all?"

He straightened. "Will that be all? Will that be all, you say?" He looked at her fat cheeks, at her small eyes. "You mean it have something nastier than pig in this place? Eh?" He brought his face down once more, almost touching hers. "Why you didn't say that all the time?" Then his gaze fell on the piece of meat lying tauntingly on the counter. His rage narrowed. He paid the money, his eyes still on the meat. Then he snatched it roughly and held it up. "Okay, Pork, is time to leave now. We spend enough time here. We have important things to do." He rushed out of the meat market.

Ramjohn pursed his lips in anticipation of her reaction. The little bitch. I will show she. I will show all of them. Today Ramjohn mean business and just let anybody cross he path. Bitches. On all side.

He spread the meat on the table, looking slyly in her direction. "Where the chopping board?" he asked in a high-pitched voice. "And the knife and the seasoning?" He heard cupboard doors being opened in the kitchen. She returned with a knife and an assortment of bottled herbs. He took the knife. "Okay, Mr. Pork, is time to begin surgery. You prepared? You have any second thoughts?" He saw with delight the shock on her face. "All right, Mr. Pork, today you have a date with Ramjohn belly."

From the corner of the kitchen she said, "I never realized that you ate pork."

"Why?" Ramhohn asked in a well-rehearsed voice. "My system not good enough for pork? Something wrong with me?"

"No . . . I just thought that your religion . . ."

"Religion? What religion? You ever listen to my name carefully? Ram and John, what religion is that? Anyways," he continued with more honesty, "I is not any Muslim. I convert years ago." But he didn't tell her that he could never bring himself to even think of eating a part of a pig.

He chopped, seasoned, and cooked, attempting to restrain his rising nausea. Then it was finished. He placed the cooked meat into his mouth, his hands shaking. Already the nourishing, energetic rage had faded, leaving him with just a dry, unserviceable irritation. It was too late. He chewed, his tongue circling, probing, feeling the texture of the meat, collecting the hot juices flowing out. The meat felt alive in his mouth, pulsing, writhing, encircling, clutching his tongue with its own desire. He saw her standing at the refrigerator, looking at him circumspectly. He turned on her. He needed something on which to anchor his diminishing anger. "What the hell you looking at? You never see a man eating pork before, eh?" She ran her hand over the refrigerator door, her fingers resting on the handle. Her silence bothered him. "You find that so strange?" He swallowed with a great heaving effort. "Run fast and call up the newspaper and them. Tell them that it have a man eating pork in an apartment." She walked slowly to the couch and sat, crossing her legs, looking at the blank television set. Ramjohn understood her measured imperturbability. "What happen, you still here? You know how much papers that will sell? 'Pork eater finally located.'" The television came on with a click. He raised his voice above its volume. "Porkman. They could call me *that*. Strange visitor from another planet. Porkton. They could call it *that*. Look! Look!" he shouted, pointing to the ceiling. "Is a bird! Is a plane! No . . . no, is only Porkman."

When he realized that she was beyond his anger, his hand once more fell to the plate and he returned his attention to the meat before him. He ate slowly, trying to give the meat indeterminate qualities, trying to convert his own chewing into an abstract act unconnected to him. Thoughts formed: first you chew thirty-two times, then swallow, then the meat pass through the esophagus, then slip down the intestines and then land up someplace in the belly. Simple. But the meat clung to him, refusing to be abstracted, refusing to divest itself of its power. It throbbed and quivered all the way down his throat. An image formed. Of his skin and flesh suddenly made transparent. And he saw himself like an X-ray image, with the meat coursing down his throat, filtering through his body. Anatomical accuracy failed. The meat was moving indiscriminately, venturing into unacceptable areas, attaching itself to his heart, spreading through his lungs, pushing against his kidneys, vaulting athletically between his veins, sprinting up to his brain. He felt dizzy. And while this dizziness brought its own nausea, it granted him a reprieve: he was now able to place his fork to his mouth, accept the matter, chew, and swallow, all with a great despairing tiredness.

He stared at the empty plate. Watching as if through a heavy cotton curtain, he saw her outline gazing silently at the television. Something tugged at his stomach. He took a deep breath. It tugged again, resisting, rising, growing. "Oh God, oh God," he bawled as he rushed to the toilet and plunged his finger down his throat. Chunk after tiny chunk came up. He was surprised at the quantity he had eaten. He pushed his finger deeper, wagging and twisting, insistent that nothing escape. He rose and lowered his head to the sink, allowing the water to fall over his head. He took one of her pink towels from the rack and wiped his head, watching the baldness, which he had camouflaged by packing all his hair on the brown spot, suddenly exposed. He took one of her spiky brushes and brushed, repacking.

He left the toilet, slowly closing the door. He walked purposefully, removed the imaginary curtain, leaned against an imaginary door jamb, and observed her staring at the television, her face expressionless. He said softly, "Okay, you could go to the newspaper now and give them this headline. Tell them to write this: 'Pork win battle. Man submit.'" Sarcasm failed. He was too tired. Her eyes were focused on the screen. He followed her gaze. The host's artificial hair curled articulately over his forehead. "The Caribbean islands, yours for a month. Just imagine that!" Women in the audience screamed, young girls yelled. An idyllic scene interrupted. A sun-laden seashore. Light blue waves rolling beguilingly. A seagull cutting across the picture, down into the water with grace, not returning, the scene fading. More screams and yells, restrained now by awe and greed.

He sat next to her; she continued staring at the television. Something felt small and heavy in his stomach; something had eluded his finger. He studied her feet, the small curling toes, the bony ankles and the ill-fitting jeans, creased, wrinkled, not hiding or disguising shape but denoting its absence. The voice from the television filtered through, " . . . the correct answer and this dream can be yours." He thought: Dreaming of going and dreaming of returning. Everybody dreaming. Nobody waking. He was once more drawn by the neutrality of her appearance. Revealing nothing, hiding nothing. She brought her foot up onto the couch and placed her tiny forefinger on her knee, scratching. The gesture was not meant for him, said nothing. But he was touched. A small piece of meat still in his stomach moved. He asked her suddenly, "You ever think about getting pregnant?"

The host, his polished effeminacy shining through his smile, crooned, " . . . a chance to get away from it all."

After about forty seconds she clicked off the set.

And Ramjohn made several vows.

STUBBORN BONES

Karen Smythe

A merry heart doeth good like a medicine: but a broken spirit drieth the bones.
—Proverbs 17:22

FRIDAY, 10 P.M.
Marta's not in mourning, she's in love.

Dressed in a tightly belted blue jersey shift, and wearing sunglasses, she met me at Union Station. She was easy to pick out because of her height — with heels, she is taller than you, remember? — and that water-falling hair, the colour of cornsilk in the sun, could belong to no one else. I expected her to look washed out — weary, at least — but she was smiling as we approached each other. The dark glasses pointed gently upwards at the corners and gave Marta a sly, stylish look. They were not a disguise for sadness.

I felt dowdy, drained, my skin dried by the static air of the rail car. Marta hugged me close, her long arms cradling me as if I were a doll, and said, "I'm so happy — so happy you are here! I want you to meet him."

At first I thought that she meant to take me to the funeral home, to see her father (whom I'd never met), and that she was still speaking about him in the present tense because he had died so suddenly.

"Dad's best friend has been a big help to me."

Ah, so that's it, I thought. I know her codes. I've heard of people making love in cemeteries, but sending perfumed glances over your father as he takes his last breath? Only Marta could displace grief for a gamble; only Marta, from across the hospital bed, could look through the tangle of tubes into the eyes of a stranger and tell him, without speaking, "I wouldn't say no."

You would say I'm being too hard on M., that she should take pleasure where she finds it. Why not? You always did. Better sorry than safe, that was your motto. And how many times I heard you say you were sorry! So often that I craved your absence, finally, more than anything in the world. But I used to believe you, gullible girl that I was; I even believed that you really were comforting a brokenhearted Marta one night when I found you embracing on the patio. Yet here I am, going to her, because it seems the right thing to do for such an old friend. Only this time, someone else's husband is comforting dear M.

SATURDAY, NOON

You'd like her apartment. Spare furniture with clean lines and white walls. Sofa a decent enough bed for my well-travelled bones.

M. is in the shower — singing, if you can believe it — but will be ready as soon as she dries her hair. Visitation is this afternoon and I don't know how M. will cope. She hasn't cried yet, at least not in front of me.

Marta was not close to him, hardly ever saw her father after her parents divorced; but she was named executor in his will. What a word — as if the dead die again when the remnants of their lives are divvied, disputed, dispersed.

When I was thirteen, Father showed me where he kept his will, so I'd know what to do in case the plane he and Mother were taking to Europe were to crash in the Atlantic. As he pulled the envelope from his desk drawer, I was proud and also mortified. It was as though by hinting at death, my parents were inviting it, as though by involving me in the business of dying they were changing my life forever.

At breakfast I asked Marta if she had any unfinished business with her dad. She lifted her face and said, "Jerome and I — it's not a father thing, if that's what you're thinking. I've worked it out. I never even had a father around when I grew up, so how could it be that?"

I looked at our reflections on her black lacquer tabletop, my face stretched out, hers upside down, and I finished my toast. Then she asked after you and I wanted to be gone, anywhere else. I haven't told anyone back home that I left you, and I don't think I want Marta to be the first to know.

SATURDAY, 5 P.M.
At the funeral parlour today, M. greeted visitors with Jerome at her side, and I swear it could have been the receiving line at their wedding. Jerome is a little taller than M.; he is slight, grey-haired, but has fine features so his face doesn't look his age: it is soft, almost feminine. Reminds me of that actor, you know — his name is on the tip of my tongue. Anyhow, they smiled, introduced

people to each other, and circulated. "Coffee, anyone?" M. said, barely hiding, barely trying to hide her joy. I avoided Jerome because I didn't want to say, "Pleased to meet you," when I wasn't.

I was glad to leave, around 4 o'clock. There were a lot of people, friends of her father, whose name, by the way, was Henrick. The casket was open. He looked a little like Marta (she looks like him, I should say), and he looked not so much dead as unreal. They had put so much pancake makeup on him — to cover the marks where his head hit the steps, all the way down from the top of the stairs, where his heart stopped — that his face had the sheen of Silly Putty. That colour, too, of new putty before the cartoon ink is picked up and worked through the pinky beige, darkening it.

The whole time we were there I heard the director's adding machine clicking, like a slot machine, in the front office. This is the kind of detail I know you'd appreciate, see the humour in, even.

We came back here to change and M. said, "Come to Jerome's with me. His wife is away and we'll have dinner together." She had her overnight bag in her hand.

SATURDAY, 11 P.M.
We had wine before dinner. Jerome leaned over to refill my glass and then kept his back to Marta while he asked me questions, the first of which was, "What brings you to Toronto?" I thought he must be joking, but he seemed to be serious. I could see Marta's mane behind Jerome's head, a golden backdrop for his performance — not as the best friend, grieving, but the lover.

Because I was bored, I kept imagining his wife would walk in, a powerful woman bursting in to upend the stage and tear down the scenery. Jerome and Marta were not worried. In fact, they acted as if they were the married couple and even argued over how much wine Jerome had poured for himself while we chatted.

I remember deliberately not arguing with you over anything, at first, because I knew you'd just come from a miserable marriage with broken dishes and slammed doors and great silences. I knew you didn't need me, either, and I didn't want to risk moving from shaky ground to a gully.

But later, there were times when I lost my hold and would tell you my fears. Then you would turn away, saying, "There are no guarantees," and "It's better this way, we won't go stale." And then I think I hated you, you and your philosophical footwork. I can see myself enraged and devastated — standing in the kitchen, hands gripping the counter, sobbing into the tea-stained sink. All my jealous anger and grief and bruised, untimely love poured out of me. The sight of your back that night was enough to break mine, to break *me*.

The episode was an excuse for your leaving, and you stayed away for weeks. I called Marta only an hour after you were gone. She slept on our sofa for a few days. Then she would leave messages on our machine for me to come home to, so I wouldn't feel so alone in the world. She'd say, "Hi, it's me. Just going to sleep so I thought I'd say goodnight," or, "Guess you are out. Oh well, I'm thinking of you, sweetie!" or, "Call me when you're home. I'll be here!" Things like that. The daily routine of our lives was reported, recorded —

shared little reminders that we were important to each other.

Jerome helped to cook the meal tonight. M. donned an apron as soon as we arrived and made herself right at home; and I, in short, did my sociable best throughout dinner. We all seemed so efficient at happiness, and no mention was made of Henrick, none at all. Then M. said, "We'll drive you back." They had done their best, too, and I was in the way. Thirty-two hours on the train, and I was in their way.

Oh, it's late. Too late; now my eyes are heavy but my mind stays awake, and the funeral is at ten in the morning (why are they always morning affairs?). I think I'll change my ticket and leave in the afternoon. Why wait till Tuesday, now? Marta is not alone.

SUNDAY, 3 P.M.

Riding the rails again. I was so eager to climb back aboard today, knowing that I will be home in my own bed tomorrow. I thought of Buster Keaton's *The Railrodder* this morning, his silly slapstick adventure. Hilarious, but he never smiles, does he? As he travels down the tracks and across the country, everything he does seems sad and graceful. He tucks a white linen napkin under his bowtie, and the wind blows it upward, covering his face. In the morning, while the car sways and tilts and bumps along, he manages still to pour, from a silver service into a china cup, his morning tea. Oblivious to weather, to time, to place, he pulls all he needs from a bottomless bin — trying to establish the habits of home, on a moving vehicle, in an unknown land. I always thought that was not so much to ask for, routine. Yet you, my uncharted territory, you resisted such mapping. By me, at least, though invisible ink might have done the trick.

SUNDAY, 10 P.M.

There is something very dismal about underground train stations: entombed, vault-like, gritty as bomb shelters. I can imagine Paris, 1940 — desperate people scurrying in the sewers with gunfire around them sounding like knuckles cracking over and over, the echoes hollow and amplified, and bullets sparking off the cement walls.

Remember our honeymoon tour of the catacombs? The humidity suffocated me, tepid water dripping from the lime-lined, too-low ceilings lined with occasional wire-covered bulbs lighting so dimly the slow way down those narrow corridors that seemed to be closing in like a vise. The sign said, in English, "You are now entering the Empire of the Dead" — and then the thick walls of skulls and femurs, arranged in perfect patterns, with signs noting years of plagues and floods and the need for this place, for the undertaker's underworld.

I looked at the millions of bones and thought how willful they are, how stubborn.

It was the usual sermon at Henrick's funeral, about the better world that awaits, and how God takes a life for his own dark reasons sometimes. The minister called him Henry. I sat at the back, in case the service ran late (I didn't want to risk missing my train). Marta sat at the front of the chapel in the family pew with the family few (two cousins, Marta's mother, and her father's aunt).

Jerome joined them after the service began. Head high, he glided down the aisle in a sharply pressed grey suit, making a big show of being quiet, and squeezed between M. and the great aunt, who was too distraught to notice his arrival.

I saw M. turn her eyes from the minister to Jerome, as he approached her. I saw her beam under the broad rim of her black felt hat as she kissed the air with her glossy reddened lips and drew him to her, inhaling deeply.

MONDAY, 11 A.M.

I didn't sleep well last night. First, the blanket the steward gave me was in a plastic bag, and when I took it out I smelled Nan. The nursing home must have laundered its bedclothes in the same institutional detergent, I suppose.

Nan always said she missed my grandfather most when she got into bed at night with the lights off, the sheets cold and crisp. By morning she had used the whole bed, warming it, but waking alone was always a little new, she said, and she never got used to it. I thought I'd be sparing myself such pain, breaking from you before we'd grown old together.

I dozed off and on but was wakened each time we passed through a town — not by the grinding of the brakes, or by the jolts of the engine stopping and starting, but by the lights along the tracks, which were so bright that they pierced the window blind and my eyelids, too. Each time it happened I was confused, thinking I was still at Marta's, but then I would remember that Jerome was probably with her instead.

To energize myself I decided to indulge in a sit-down breakfast. This took courage, because I'm frightened of walking between the cars — those moving pieces of metal, overlapping to make a floating floor, just don't seem stable to me. They remind me of the bends in straws you get in hospitals: jointed like a lobster's claw but, bent too often, they lose their shape and finally break apart.

I ordered one egg, over easy. The package of pepper tore and I spilled so much on the plate that it looked like an ashtray. That, and the mist outside the window, gave me a sudden craving for the smell of your hair. When we'd shower together the cigarette scent was released by the steam; tiny beads of water would settle on every strand and make you look angel-kissed, unearthly.

If you were here, this trip would be exciting. We would dine in the dark on exotic CN fare after the last call. You can make even bologna seem sensuous. Even this scratchy grey blanket would be soft if we shared it — and the rhythm of the train, its blues-call whistle, reminds me of you, too . . .

A woman in her seventies is sitting next to me this trip. Last night, when I really wanted to read myself to sleep, I listened to her talk about friends she'd made during her train travels. I had to fake a smile for two hours straight. She smiled, too, as she told her stories. Smiled through tales of a woman from Vancouver who had become a close friend afterwards, through letters, over the years. Then this friend had written to her asking for help, after a domestic catastrophe of some kind, and she told me — still smiling! — that she never answered, and had thankfully not heard from her since.

"Friendship has its limits," she said, nodding.

You said that our love had its limits, too. Because of me, you said. Because I'm so stubborn and because I would rather be right than happy. Well, my dear, you were dead-on about that, then; but now? Having just done the "right" thing and made no one — not Marta, not myself — happy, I have to wonder what it would be like to meet you again, to try happiness instead of safety.

I can almost see you strutting across the platform to greet me. (You *do* strut, you know! I was always struck by your gallant gait: shoulders braced, arms straight at your side — those solid arms, taut-muscled, thick like clay. You walk with your chest displayed as if adorned with badges of honour won in some distant battle, as if you had inhaled and refused to let go of the breath.)

If only you could read these pages, you would know what my fingers mean should they ever squeeze yours again. Then you would know what my stubborn bones want.

I hear the foghorns in the harbour — like great whale-cries, wired for sound. What power in those subtle bellows, those echoes across the miles, murmured to their own.

MELODY

Lisa Moore

- 1 -

MELODY LETS THE FIRST HALF-DOZEN CARS GO BY; SHE says she has a bad feeling about them. The trip will take as long as it takes, she says. There are no more cars for an hour. She gets her cigarettes out of her jean jacket and some matches from the El Dorado. We had been dancing there last night until the owner snapped on the lights. The band immediately aged; they could have been our parents. They wore acid-washed jeans and T-shirts that said *Arms Are For Hugging, Viva la Sandinista;* and *Feminist? You Bet!!!*

Outside the El Dorado two mangy Camaros, souped up for the weekend Smash-Up Derby, revved their engines and tore out of the parking lot. I watched their tail lights swerve and bounce in the dark. They dragged near the mall and sparks lit the snagged fenders. A soprano yelp of rubber and then near silence. I could smell the ocean far beyond the army barracks. The revolving Kentucky Fried Chicken bucket still glowing in the pre-dawn light. Waves shushing the pebble beach; Brian Fiander falling in beside me. He had been downing B-52s. He was lanky and discombobulated until his big hand clasped my shoulder and his too-long limbs snapped into place like the poles of a pup tent.

*

The clock radio in my dorm room comes on in the early afternoon and I listen to the announcer slogging through the temperatures across the island. Twenty-nine degrees. Mortification and the peppery sting of a fresh crush. I'd let Brian Fiander hold my wrists over my head against the brick wall of the dorm while he kissed me; his hips thrusting with a lost, intent zeal, the dawn sky as pale and grainy as sugar. Brian Fiander knew what he was doing. The recognition of his expertise made my body ting and smoulder. My waking thought: I have been celebrated.

I feel logy and grateful. Also sophisticated. I'd had an orgasm, though I didn't know it at the time. I didn't know *that's* what that was. I could count on one hand the number of times I'd said the word out loud, though I'd read about it. I believed myself to be knowledgeable on the subject. I'd closed my eyes while Brian touched me and what I'd felt was like falling asleep, except in the opposite direction and at alarming speed: falling awake. Wildly alert. Falling into myself.

I make my way down the corridor to the showers, the stink of warming SpaghettiOs wafting from the kitchenette. Wavy Fagan passes me in her cotton candy slippers and she smirks. I have a crowbar grin; his hand on my breast, slow, sly circles. Wavy smirks and I know, *Oh that's what that was.*

The showers are full of fruity mist. Brenda Parsons brushing her teeth, her glasses steamed. She turns toward me blindly, her mouth foaming toothpaste. She had been going out with Brian Fiander.

*

We can see anything that's coming long before it arrives and nothing's coming. The highway rolls in the sulky haze of mid-afternoon and Melody and I are eternally stuck to the side of it. The night before comes back in streaks. A glass smashing, swimming spotlights, red, blue. Hands, zippers. The truck, when it appears, is a lisping streak, there and not there, as it dips into the valleys. A black truck parting the quavering heat. A star of sunlight reaming the windshield. I say, Do I stick my thumb out or what?

I'll do the thinking, says Melody. She ties the jean jacket around her waist in a vicious knot. We don't hitch, but the truck pulls over anyway. I run down the highway and open the door. Melody stays where she is, just stands, smoking.

My friend is coming, I say. I climb up onto the bouncy seat. The guy is a hunk. A Happy Face on his sweatshirt. Smoky sunglasses. Brian Fiander barely crosses my mind. Brian is too willing and skinny; he's unworthy of me.

This guy tilts the rear-view mirror and puts his hand over the stick shift, which vibrates like the pointer of a Ouija board. He has a wedding ring, but he can't be more than twenty. A plain gold band. The fine hair on his fingers is blonde and curls over the ring, catching the light, and I almost lean toward him so that he'll touch my cheek with the back of his hand.

I've had too much sun, and I may still be drunk from the night before. Is that possible? I experience a glimmer of clairvoyance as convincing as the smell of exhaust. I close my eyes and the shape of the windshield floats on my eyelids, bright violet with a chartreuse trim. I know in an instant and without doubt that I will marry, never be good with plants, suffer incalculable loss that almost, almost tips me over, but I will right myself. I will forget Melody completely, but she will show up and something about her as she is now — her straight defiant back in the rear-view — will be exactly the same. She'll give me a talisman and disappear as unexpectedly as she came.

Melody is still standing with her cigarette, holding one elbow. She's looking down the road, her back to us, the wind blowing a zigzag part in her hair. A faint patch of sweat on her pink shirt like a Rorschach test between her shoulder blades.

She finally drops the cigarette and crushes it under her sneaker. She walks toward the truck with her head bent down, climbs up beside me, and pulls the door shut. She doesn't even glance at the driver.

Skoochie over, she says. My arm touches the guy's bare arm and I feel the heat of his sunburn, a gliding muscle as he puts the truck in gear.

We all set? the guy asks.

We're ready, I say. There's a pine-tree air freshener, a pouch of tobacco on the dash, an apple slice to keep it fresh, smells as pristine as the South Pole. It's going to rain. Melody changes the radio station, hitting knots of static. The sky goes dark, darker, darker and the first rumble is followed by a solid, thrilling crack. A blur of light low and flickering. The rain tears into the pavement like a racing pack of whippets. Claws scrabbling over the top of the cab. Livid grey muscles of rain.

*

Melody and I are working on math in my dorm room. She kisses me on the mouth. Later, for the rest of my life, while washing dishes, jiggling drops of rain hanging on the points of every maple leaf in the window, or in a meeting when someone writes on a flow chart and the room fills with the smell of Magic Marker — during those liminal non-moments fertile with emptiness — I will be overtaken by swift, half-formed collages of memory. A heady disorientation, seared with pleasure, jarring. Among those memories: Melody's kiss. Because it was a kiss of revelatory beauty. I realized I had never initiated anything in my life. Melody acted; I was acted upon.

I'm not like that, I say, gay or anything.

No big deal, she smiles. She twists an auburn curl around in her finger, supremely unruffled. Aplomb. She's showing me how it's done.

I like you and everything, I say.

Relax, she says. She turns back to the math, engaging so quickly that she solves the problem at once.

*

What I feel on the side of the highway, ozone in the air, the epic sky: I am falling hugely in love. Hank, the guy who picked us up in his black truck. Brian Fiander. Melody. Myself. Whomever. A hormonal metamorphosis, the unarticulated lust of a virgin, as errant, piercing, and true as lightning. A half-hour later the truck hydroplanes.

Hank slams on the brakes. The truck spins in two weightless circles. I hear the keening brakes of the eighteen-wheeler coming toward us, ploughing a glorious wave of water in front of it. The sound as desperate and restrained as a whale exhausted in a net. I can see the grill of the eighteen-wheeler's cab through the sloshing wave like a row of monster teeth. The transport truck stops close enough, our bumpers almost touching.

After a long wait, the driver steps down from the cab. He stands beside his truck, steely points of rain spiking off his shoulders like medieval armour. Melody opens her door and steps down. She walks toward the driver, but veers to the side of the road and throws up.

The driver of the transport truck catches up with her there. When Melody has finished puking he turns her toward him, resting his hands on her shoulders. She speaks and hangs her head. He begins to talk, admonishing, cajoling; once bending his head back and looking up into the rain. He chuckles. The thick film of water sloshing over the windshield makes their bodies wiggle like sun-drugged snakes. After a while, he lifts her chin. He takes a handkerchief from an inside pocket and shakes it out and holds it at arm's-length, examining both sides. He hands it to her and she wipes her face.

I'm not responsible for this, Hank whispers. He lays his hand on the horn.

Melody gets back in the truck. She's shivering. The other driver climbs into his cab. His headlights come on. The giant lights splinter into needles of pink and blue and violet and the rain is visible in the broad arms of light. As the truck pulls away the lights dim and narrow, as if the transport truck has cunning. Then it drives away. Hank takes off his sunglasses, folds the arms, and places them in a holder for sunglasses glued to the dash. He moves his hand over his face, down and up, then rests his forehead on the wheel. He holds the wheel tight.

What did you say to him? Hank asks. He waits for Melody to answer, but she doesn't. Finally, he lifts his head. He flings his arm over the back of the seat so that he can turn the truck and I see, without his sunglasses, the crackle of lines at the corners of his eyes.

*

I watch Melody inside the Irving station a couple of hours later. Her pink sleeveless blouse through the window amid the reflections of the pumps and the black truck I'm leaning against; she passes through my reflection and, returning to the counter, passes through me again like a needle sewing something up. Hank opens the hood and pulls out the dipstick. He takes a piece of paper towel from his back pocket, draws it down the length of stick, stopping it from wavering. I realize he's trembling.

Melody comes out with a bottle of orange juice. It has stopped raining. Steam lifts off the asphalt and floats into the trees. The sunlight is elegiac. Sky, Canadian flag, child with red shirt — all mirrored in the glassy water on the pavement at our feet. A car passes and the child's reflection is a crazy red flame breaking apart under the tires. The juice in Melody's hand has an orange halo. A brief rainbow arcs over the wet forest behind the Irving station.

You married, Hank? Melody asks. He's still fiddling with things under the hood.

I believe I met you at the El Dorado, Melody says.

Hank unhooks the hood, lowers it, and lets it drop. He rubs his hands in the paper towel, and gives her a look.

I don't think so, he says.

I believe you bought me a drink, Melody says.

You're most likely thinking of someone else, he says.

Could have sworn it was me, Melody says. It sure felt like me. She laughs and it comes out a honk.

I'm going to carry on by myself from here, Hank says.

But you're probably right, Melody says. The guy I'm thinking of wasn't wearing a ring.

Good luck, he says. Melody hefts herself up into a stack of white plastic lawn chairs next to a row of barbecues and swings her legs. Hank gets in his truck and pulls out onto the highway.

I can take care of myself, Melody yells. But now we've lost our ride, and it'll take a good hour to get to the clinic in Corner Brook.

*

The nurse leans against the examining table with her arms folded under her clipboard.

You'll need your mother's signature, she says. Anyone under nineteen needs permission from a parent or guardian. You'll need to sit before a board of psychiatrists in St. John's to prove you're fit.

Tears slide fast to Melody's chin and she raises a shoulder and rubs her face roughly against the collar of her jean jacket.

She wouldn't sign, Melody says.

The nurse turns from Melody and pulls a paper cone from a dispenser and holds it under the water cooler. A giant wobbling bubble works its way up, breaking at the surface. It sounds like a cooing pigeon, dank and maudlin. I can hear water rat-a-tatting from a leaky eavestrough onto a metal garbage lid.

My mother has fourteen children, Melody says.

The nurse drinks the water and crunches the cup. She touches the lever on the garbage bucket with her white shoe and the lid smacks against the wall. She tosses the cup and it hits the lid and falls inside. Then she wipes her forehead with the back of her hand.

You can forge the signature and I'll witness it, she says. She takes the top off the Bic pen with her teeth. She flicks a few pages and shows Melody where to sign. Melody signs and the nurse signs below.

I don't need to tell you, the nurse says.

I appreciate it, says Melody.

*

That year I live on submarine sandwiches microwaved in plastic wrap. When I peel back the wrap, the submarine hangs out soggy and spent. The oozing processed cheese hot enough to raise blisters. I wear a lumber jacket over cheesecloth skirts, with red Converse sneakers. I've learned to put a speck of white make-up in the outer corner of my eyes to give me a vaguely astonished look. On Valentine's Day, in the dorm elevator, I tear an envelope; dried rose petals fall out and whirl in the updraft of the opening elevator doors and there is Brian Fiander. I see I was wrong; he isn't skinny. If he still wants me, he can have me. I will do whatever Brian Fiander wants and if he wants to dump me afterward, as he has with Brenda Parsons, he can go right ahead. He seems to go through girls pretty quickly and I want to be gone through.

*

Melody and I get tickets on the CN bus into St. John's for the abortion. I wait for her outside a boardroom in the Health Sciences. I catch a glimpse of the psychiatrists, five men seated in a row behind a table. Melody comes out a half-hour later.

What did they say? I ask.

One of them commented on my hat, she says. He said I must think myself pretty special with a fancy hat. He asked if I thought I was pretty special.

What did you say?

The same smile as when she kissed me. Learning to smile like that will take time. Aplomb takes time. The rainbow must belong to some other story. Stretching over the hills behind the Irving station, barely there.

After the abortion I hold her hand. She's lying on a stretcher and she reaches a hand out over the white sheet, which is tucked so tightly around her shoulders that she has to squirm to get her arm free.

Not too bad, she says. She is eerily ashen. Tears move from the corners of her eyes to her ears.

Sometimes you have to do things, she says.

*

During the rest of the winter I spend a lot of time with Wavy Fagan. She's marrying her high school woodworking teacher; they have to keep the relationship secret. Wavy smokes, holding the cigarette out the window. I fan the fire alarm with her towel.

I don't spend much time with Melody; time with her is exhausting. Wavy smokes, and she taps the window with her hard fingernail and tells me to come look. Six floors below, Melody is crossing the dark parking lot. It's snowing and a white circle of snow has gathered in the brim of her hat and it glows under the streetlight.

She's the one had the abortion for Hank Mercer, Wavy says.

- 2 -

I am drunk and in profound pain. My tooth. I am a forty-year-old widow in someone else's bed. Whose bed? Robert turns on the bedside light. Primrose Place is where I am. Robert's new house with new everything. Big housewarming party. I can feel the throb of it through the floorboards. Wrought-iron this and marble that. Where I've woken up for the last eleven months. He untangles his bifocals from the lace doily on the side table and comes over to my side and gets down on his knees. He takes my cheeks in his hands. I can smell the alcohol in his sweat, on his breath.

Open up, he says.

You have to take care of it, I say.

It's five in the morning. He pays the taxi. I lean against the glass door of his office while he finds the keys. Everything behind the door leaps into its proper place just before the door swings open. The fluorescent lights flutter grey, then a bland spread of office light. The office simulates an office. A sterile environment in which to extract a tooth. Robert passes down a hall of convincing office dividers. Turns on the X-ray machine.

That's got to warm up, he says.

Just pull it out, I say.

Robert gets a small card from the receptionist's desk and slings himself into a swivel chair. The chair rolls and tips and he is flung onto the floor. He grips the desk and drags himself up and sits in the chair. He puts a pen behind his ear and feels around on the desk for it and remembers it behind his ear. The top of his head shines damply.

Any allergies, abnormal medical conditions, sexually transmitted diseases? He's slurring. I don't bother.

He leaves the room and I hear water running in a sink. The *rip rip rip* of paper towels from a dispenser. He comes back and pulls on a pair of latex gloves, letting them snap at his wrists, flexing his fingers.

Who was the man you were talking to? Robert asks.

The gloves are the smell I've noticed on his hands, like the smell of freshly watered geraniums. He takes an X-ray and leads me to the chair.

Make yourself comfortable, he says. There's a poster of rotting gums — enlarged, florid gums oozing pus, the roots of the blackened teeth exposed and bleeding. Photographs of everyone who works in the office — the other dentists, the dental hygienists and receptionists. I look for the redhead. A brief, uncomplicated affair, he said, terrific sex. Long after it was over Robert tidied away her student loan and credit card balance. Braids and a lab coat covered in teddy bears and balloons. I sink into the chair and a moment later feel myself sink into the chair. Robert prepares a syringe. He drops it. He picks it up and looks at the tip. He scrutinizes the tip of the needle for some time.

That man was all over you, he says.

I'm allowed to have a conversation.

He tosses the syringe toward the garbage pail; it hits the wall and bounces end over end across the room. Robert holds up one finger.

I'll get another one.

You do that, Robert. I can hardly open my mouth. He puts his hands on my face and leans in to look, his entire weight rests on my sore cheek. He steadies himself and he straightens up.

The infection is too severe, he says.

Coward.

We should run a course of antibiotics first.

Robert, please.

This is unethical, he says. I love you. He begins to sob. He sobs silently with his mouth hanging open, his shoulders curled in, cradling himself. I don't care what position I've put him in. His house with the new, leakless skylights and cedar sauna. The spacious greenhouse, pong of aggressive rose bushes, dill, peat. Asking his dinner guests to pull the pearl onions from the earth. Orchids in aquariums with timed sprinklers. Philip Glass on the sound system, building tense, cerebral crescendos. Density of pixels this, lightweight that, gigs of this, surround sound. Pull my fucking tooth, you drunken idiot.

You are so remote, he says, wiping his eyes.

If you're crying about that guy.

Don't you feel anything?

He sticks the needle into my infected gum and I dig my nails into his wrist and my heel kicks the chair. The numbing spreads up my face and partway across my upper lip. My cheek is cold and stupid and the pain is gone in less than a minute. My nails break his skin.

We'll wait until you're good and frozen, he says. He leaves the room. I hear him walk into the reception area. He crashes into something. A coffee maker starts to grumble. The smell of coffee. He turns on a radio. A woman says, That's the reality of the situation, then there is static, and finally classical music. He returns with the X-ray. He seems to have sobered up.

The bacteria think they died and went to heaven, he says. He has become reverent.

Robert, I need to know you'll stop if I ask you to. He clips the X-ray to a light board. My teeth look blue and ghostly. The white jaw bone. I think of my husband buried in the cemetery near Quidi Vidi Lake. Robert goes into the reception area. I hear him pour a coffee. He opens the drawer of a filing cabinet.

Are you good and frozen? he shouts.

*

The toothache has been mild for weeks. I think I'm awake but the bed is facing in the wrong direction. Or I'm in the wrong bed. A toilet bowl filling continuously. Wet leaves and earth — is there a window? Stenographers on squeaky keyboards wait for a breath of wind and resume. A car unzips a skim of water. Hard fingernails clicking glass, the leaves, the skylight, keying data. Data dripping from leaf tip to leaf tip. A religious cult in the sewer can be overheard whispering in the toilet bowl. A conspiracy, and the stenographers ache to crack it. Wind sloshes through the trees, and the typing subsides. The trees are just trees. I am my tooth, a monolithic grief. A man beside me. Please be Des; please be him; it *is* Des.

The beach to ourselves, the park closed, early September. What heat, so late in the season. Each wave leaves a ribbon of glare in the sand as it withdraws. The sun is low and red, scissored by the long grass. Des strips to his underwear, trots toward the water. Stands at the edge of the ocean. High up, a white gull.

Des charges, arms raised over his head, yelling. The gull is silent. So high up it's barely there. Wide circles. It dips closer. The wave's crest tinged pink, fumbling forward. He dives through the falling crest. The soles of his feet. He passes through, bobs on the other side. Flicks water from his hair. His fist flies up, wing of water under his arm. The gull screeches. Metallic squawk, claws outstretched, reaching for the sand. The sun through the grass on the hill hits the gull's eye like a laser beam, a red holograph. The gull's pupil is a long midnight corridor to some prehistoric crimson flash deep in the skull.

Water's great, he calls. My shirt, jeans, one sock stretches long. I have to hop. The sock gives up. I run hard. The wave is building beneath the bed. Except how cold. My body seizes.

Look at the one coming, Des says. The wave comes with operatic silence. Such surety, self-knowledge, so cold and meaningless and full of blasé might. I reach out my hand. Here it comes. A wave full of light, nearly transparent, lacy webbing on the underside. The ocean sucks hard on my spine. The sandy bottom drops away.

It smashes us. The bed plummets and thumps the floor. The room makes itself felt. Dresser, a housecoat on a hook. Des died four years ago of heart failure. Peanut butter jar on the floor, fridge open. Holding the knife. Smoking toast in the stuck toaster. The red light of the ambulance on the walls of the hallway. Now I am awake.

*

Tequila I drank, scotch. Elasticized top and sarong. Beer. Robert warned me about, when he throws a party. Dancing. Slamming doors, laughter, the Stones. I have dated since Des died no one, an air traffic controller, a very young painter, no one, the reporter guy, absolutely no one, the carpenter. The tooth started two days ago. I didn't tell Robert. Pleased to meet you, hope you guess my name. You can't leave. How can you leave? Bodies pressed close, smoky ceiling. Blow the speakers. We took a cab. Hope you guess my. Get a taxi. If we dance. In the fridge door. Mine are the cold ones. Pleased to meet you. Have one of mine. The cold ones. I got laid. Tell me. I'll tell you after this. We need a toast. Our coats are where? Forget the coats. Don't leave, it's a party. Because the toilet. What happened to the tequila? Your own stupid fault. My wife took the traditional route. Does it have a worm in it? I'll put one in if you like. There have been women, yes. There have been women, I'll admit. We'll call ourselves the Fleshettes. The people impressed me most. I'm not responsible. Hope you guess my. We haven't talked. We're talking now. This is talking? Name. I love you. Don't say that. I love you, what do you think? I think more beer.

*

The sky is the deepest blue it gets before it begins to look black. The stars are blue. The trees roar with wind and become quiet. I lie flat on my husband's grave and look at the stars. Freshly mown grass, a faint marshy smell, the ducks at the edge of the lake. This morning, resting my head against the hand dryer in the bathroom of our office. Tears start this way: the bridge of my nose, my eyelids, the whole face tingling, the clutch of a muscle in the throat. The smell of burnt coffee — homey, unloved office coffee — makes me cry. Some songs: John Prine. Bad blue icing on the birthday cake the girls bought for the boss. Anything engraved or monogrammed. Some weather: fog that carries the fishy rot of the harbour. Sirens of any kind in the distance. TV dinners. Restaurant windows with lots of couples. Clotheslines with men's underwear or infants' clothes. Putting the key in the door of my empty house after work. I cry at least four times a day. The tears catch in the plastic rims of my glasses. My eyelids like slugs. While waiting for the elevator I hear laughter inside, ascending, inclusive, sexual. I cry with jealousy. Prissy Andrews coming into the bathroom after me. Unclicking her purse, removing the wad of cotton swab from a pill bottle, tapping two pills into my hand. Prissy smoothing her thumbs over my wet cheeks. She turns me to the mirror and she looks hard at me.

Lipstick will give you a whole new lease, she says.

I can't be alone, I say.

The leaves smell leathery, pumpkinish. The branches creak when the wind rubs them together. Des's hands folded over a rose, wedding ring. When do the teeth fall away from the skull? Does that happen? It's beginning to get cold. Snow on his headstone makes me panicky.

A flashlight waves erratically through the shrubs, catching the bright green moss on a carved angel's cheek, her cracked wing. Another flashlight, soft oval bouncing in the leaves overhead, scuffle of feet. I'm surrounded by a circle of teenagers with baseball bats and fence pickets. They step, one by one, out of the trees and bushes. Or else they have always been standing there. All the headstones, tipping, lichen-crusted. I stand up, my legs watery. We stand like that, not speaking or moving.

You seen a guy run through here?

No, I whisper. I haven't seen anybody. Three police men arrive and the teenagers flee. A policeman steps forward and puts an arm around my shoulder and I cry into his armpit.

*

Robert lowers a tool into my mouth and I say, Stop.

That was a test, I say.

He says, That was a scalpel. I would just trust me if I were you.

I feel him cut the gum and fold the flesh back. His eyes full of veins, blue and violet; my blood sprays dots on his glasses. He takes up another instrument and tugs at the tooth, twisting it, and I feel it tearing away. The hoarse, sputtering noise of the suction hose removing blood and saliva. Robert worked for nothing in Colombia after he graduated, teaching the revolutionaries to be dentists, the distant spitting of gunfire in the fields beyond his classroom. During the dot-com boom he invested — in and out — unspeakably rich.

My tooth hits a chrome bowl with a bright ping. He begins to sew the stitches. I feel the thread move through the gum and the sensation, though painless, nauseates me. Three tight stitches, the side of my mouth puckered.

He gives me a wad of cotton and tells me to bite down. He peels the latex gloves. I worry the loose ends of the stitches with my wooden tongue. They feel like ingrown cat whiskers.

I've wanted to ask for some weeks, Robert says.

Maybe this is not the best time, I say.

I want to marry you, he says.

*

The sound of the sliding metal rings when I rip open the shower curtain unnerves me. Waiting for the toaster to pop, a butter knife in my hand, I am aware of a presence. The washer shimmies across the laundry room floor until it works the plug from the wall and the motor goes quiet. The water stops slushing. An engrossing, animate silence. Every object — the vacuum cleaner, a vase of dried thistles — has become sensitive. The fridge knows. The unmade bed is not ordinary. I put a glass down and check. It's exactly where I set it down. Loving a dead person takes immense energy and it makes me cry.

*

Robert works the champagne cork with his thumbs. The cork bounces off the ceiling and hits a mirror causing a web of cracks. He hands me my glass and I can feel the fizz on my face.

He says, This is the happiest day of my life.

We twine arms and drink and with the awkward intimacy of this, the complete lack of irony, I know instantly I've made a mistake.

*

Robert is still at work and I'm watching the decorating channel. The camera roves slowly over an empty, palatial house in Vermont. A woman's chipper voice: Here we have an oak table, very countryish, but *workable* chairs. This dining room absolutely screams to be used. Use me, it's screaming!

I turn off the TV and listen to the shrill nothing that fills Robert's house. Leaves swirl off the lawn in twisting columns. A brown leaf hits the glass and sticks. The starlings are flying in formation over the university. A darkening, black cloud draws together and becomes thin as they change direction. The sky is full of grey lustre and the starlings seem feverish. I remember Des parking by the duck pond once, just to watch them. It was late, we had groceries — ice cream in the trunk.

They're just playing, he said. I want to stay here, don't you?

I think: If you are there, get in touch with me now. I believe suddenly that he can, that it is just a matter of my asking.

The phone rings at exactly that instant. It rings and rings and rings. Then it stops. I put my hand on the receiver and I can feel a warm thrum. Then it rings again, loudly. I go upstairs and brush my teeth. I rinse the brush, and start flossing. The phone rings again. It's ringing in all the rooms, terrifying me. I pour a bath and get in and when it's deep enough I put my ears under the water.

*

Robert gives me a glass of scotch and drops into the chair beside me. He presses his watch face so that the dial glows, sending a circle of green light zigzagging across his face. The sale of my house has come through. A young couple with a Dalmatian. Most of the furnishings went to the Sally Ann. A closet full of Des's shirts; a key ring with a plastic telescope, inside which there is a picture of Des and me on vacation in Mexico. It has to be held to a light. We are laughing, drinking from coconut shells. I'd let all the plants die. Robert has everything we need.

You're tired, I say. We're both tired.

What do you think of stem cell research? he asks.

There are the dishes.

I could take a hair out of your head and make another you.

The laundry is—

Two of you. The real you and another you.

I know I'm tired.

One you is a roomful already.

I can't have sex with you tonight, if that's what you're thinking, I say.

Why would I be thinking a thing like that?

I'm drifting to sleep while he talks. I dream that I say I want my real husband, and I don't know whether I've spoken out loud or not. I believe that Des is in the chair beside me and things are as they were five years ago, as if the past can do that. Lay itself down on the present. Cover it over. Become the present, even briefly. A pair of flip-flops. I'd stumbled and skinned my toe. Des had been hammering all day. The hammering had stopped, but the silent ringing of the hammer went on. It was late September and we went to the beach.

*

In the morning I hear a car coming up the long driveway and I leap out of bed. A dark green minivan pulls up under the trees. The windshield is opaque with the shadows of the maple trees. The van parks and a man steps out. He's wearing cream-coloured pants and a pastel shirt. He stretches and puts his hands on his hips. He helps a little girl out of the driver's side. She's wearing a white cotton dress and the skirt bells with the breeze. Finally the passenger door opens and a woman gets out. I'm standing in the upstairs window, struggling to get into my jeans. There is a wave rising within me. It's full of light. It's dull and smart and hurting my throat. Robert rolls over in the bed.

He says, Who would disturb us at this hour?

The woman is shielding her eyes against the sun with her hand and she's looking up into the bedroom window where I'm standing and I know without ever recognizing her, that it's Melody. I run down the stairs and out the back door without my shoes. I have never initiated anything in my life. I had forgotten her completely and here she is. She'll give me something.

She's exactly the same. The child is just like her. The guy holds out his hand. Melody says his name and I tell him I'm thrilled, but I forget his name. I forget the child's name but it's Jill.

I tried to call, she says, holding out her arms.

I'm married, I say. I start to cry. Melody kisses me.

I've messed up, Melody, I whisper.

You'll just have to do something about it, she says.

INSOMNIS

Christy Ann Conlin

A CAR SCREECHES INTO HER DREAM, WHERE SHE IS tiny and sitting on a sunny lily pad and then she is furious and wide-smacking-awake in the dark city night of her room as the hot rod screeches and squeals away, leaving rubber on the road, taking her precious and precarious sleep with it. The sheets are soaked and bits of far-off laughter bounce in the open window, cutting through the thick summer night, coming over from Gottingen Street, from the parking lot behind the house, from yards and sidewalks, in through the window, to the woman who won't sleep now until dawn.

The doctor supposes she has *transient* insomnia. From moving so much, she says? He laughs. Well, yes, from that too. But he means short-term insomnia. As opposed to *intermittent* — on and off — or *chronic* — constant — insomnia.

But I thought it would be better when I moved home to Nova Scotia, she whispers.

Maybe it *will* get better, he says, maybe when it's winter, when the air is cool.

Maybe not, she says. It's always worse in winter. I scrape at the windowpanes. Really. And then it's not just insomnia — it's seasonal claustrophobia, too . . . winter.

Location, location, location, he laughs. Maybe you should move out of the city. Maybe you should move to a better part of the city. My diagnosis is chronic bouts of transient insomnia. Stress induced. Go to sleep . . . think about moving somewhere nicer, he whispers, his finger on her nipple.

The doctor turns his head on the pillow and his lips touch her earlobe as he exhales wet breath and slowly spreads his fingers over her neck. He murmurs a story about whitewater canoeing and stars and pretty things until he snores deeply and falls suddenly into sleep with his leg across her stomach and a sweaty hand sticking to her ribs. It's the fifth time he's found her late-night dancing and the first night she's brought him home.

Outside, a woman's shrill voice catches in the thick hot air: Here, Lister, here, kitty-kitty. A car starts in the parking lot outside. Kitty does not come and she hollers out again as the car backs up and then drives off. Kitty kitty, come in now. It's past late, Lister. Kitty, you stupid kitty, it's way past late.

The car noise grows quieter and then it's just the snoring in her ear and then more

Lister, Lister, Mister Lister

the lady's voice rising and stretching on each Lister as though Lister might be sitting in a treetop and she must throw his name up through the leaves. But outside, the cat does not come.

Inside, the snoring does not stop. She nudges the doctor awake and he snaps upright, rubs his hands through his hair. Lies back down. Pulls her to him. You should drink less coffee, he whispers.

It's always like this, she says. I am a creature of the night.

Poor you, says he. Poor creature.

Poor you, she says. What about being on-call and not sleeping?

He mutters: That's different — the hospital's air-conditioned.

His breath on her neck, hands moving slowly over every curve of her body, the heat of the night melting them together, her face pushed into the damp pillow, every part of him hot inside and outside of her. His lips on her spine, pulling her hair, her head back, her hips lifting off the bed, gasping. Shush, he whispers in her ear.

*

She sits on the back deck, her naked body drying rough with salt crystals. The smell of their sweat is acrid here, where the air is cooler, but the smell is lost as the scent of the night-bloomers rises up from her verdant garden, the fragrant evening clematis running up the chain-link fence and sealing off this urban Eden.

The cat lady calls again, each syllable so elongated that the young woman knows her hands must be cupped like a bullhorn. The voice breaks, then stops. Far-off traffic sounds drone and laughter floats over from a neighbour's rooftop balcony. She loves the city on the hot summer nights when she cannot sleep, slipping from the confines of the house, sitting outside in the dark. The house a veritable sepulchre for the winter insomniac, the snow dampening the nighttime sounds of life, when the window can't be opened, sealed in from the cold, sealed in from the world.

*

She walks quickly across the Commons. It's dangerous. She knows this. She always says *never again,* but each time she slips back, safe, into the house, she knows she will cross over again, in the dark, when it is dangerous, when the night city is alive and mysterious.

This time she had slipped into the house from the back deck and into a dress and sandals. Then quietly out the front door and down the steps, the man in her bed still asleep. The old neighbour, dark as night, dragged on a cigarette, sitting on his front step.

Evenin, he said. Shouldn't be goin out alone. You know it, girl.

She knew it. Insomnia, she said. Going to get a video.

He shook his head and she walked past him, down Maynard Street.

Then she was moving fast — as she is now moving fast, halfway across the Commons, running even though there is no one around. Scared and excited. Her sandals clipping on the path. In the winter she'd be in the tub, hoping the hot water and candles would bring sleep. There is no traffic crossing Robie Street, but a police van drives up as she steps onto the sidewalk.

Problem, miss? a cop asks. His head is shaved.

No, no problem. Shit, she thinks. Looking for my cat, she says. Lister.

Now you know, dear, it's not safe to be out in this neighbourhood at night. Cat'll show up in the morning looking for breakfast.

Do they think she would she be safer on some quiet South End street? she wonders. What they think is that they should drive her home, but she lies that she lives only a block away. And they watch her walk up Compton Street, sitting in their van, the engine purring. She waves and walks into someone's dark driveway. When the sound of the van fades off, she runs back out to the sidewalk and over to the bright lights of Quinpool Road. Dripping sweat at Video Difference — open twenty-four hours, for shift workers and insomniacs. She's looking for a movie to start the beta waves in her head, the waves that dull thought. There is no cable in the house, only a VCR. She finds *Marathon Man* — a retro movie, the girl at the cash calls it. Her hair is window-cleaner blue. The girl makes change while the young woman puts a quarter in the bubble gum machine on the counter.

She blows bubbles as she heads back across the Commons, her skin yellow under the lights of the park. In the east, the sky is lightening. Soon birds will chirp, traffic will roar, people will parallel park on the street in front of the house and she will be in bed with a stranger, searching for a few early-morning hours of sleep before she drifts through a hot day on coffee and fatigue.

Her neighbour is still out smoking as she comes shining under the street light on Maynard Street. Home. This sweat is from relief and she can smell the difference. She sees the old man from the corner, as she steps from the curb. She waves as her toes poke warm fur.

*

The old neighbour watches her, white and sweaty and kneeling on the road by the skid marks. He hobbles over and shakes his head. They pick up the big cat together;

its head lolls, neck broken, eyeballs bulging from the sockets. The woman is crying and he pats her shoulder.

Poor old Lister, he says in his low voice. Lister, my boy, you shoulda stayed in tonight . . . you know it, Lister, my poor old boy. He strokes the cat, fur soft as pussy willows.

It's hard, she cries, so hard when you can't sleep.

It is, it is, so it is, says the neighbour, patting her damp hand.

And they hear the lady calling again, over on Creighton Street, each syllable shooting out like gunfire, a tiny pause as she reloads with air and resumes, relentlessly now: *Kittykittykittykittykittykitty.* The lady is standing on her step, fat and old, wearing a green nightie and pink slippers, her hand clutching the railing as she screams. The eastern sky is forget-me-not blue as here, in the city, the summer morning breaks through the last film of night as the transient insomniac and the old black man slowly cross the street with the shattered bundle of fur and bones in their arms.

WHY MEN FISH WHERE THEY DO

Carol Bruneau

DOOLEY KINRADE HAD A PECULIAR HABIT OF SETTING THE emergency brake each and every time he hit a light. Slotted behind the wheel of his two-month-old silver Intrepid, he glanced both ways before releasing it after the light went green. Dooley, like a pilot in the cockpit, wired and edgy as a jockey at the starting gate. Even with no traffic, this being a Saturday, scarcely 6 A.M., the sun barely up — it was still too early for joggers. And it wasn't as if he was headed for the office, or court: he was going fishing, for God's sake. Dawn's dewy blush just fingering the sky as he thought of Mathilde home in bed. Dreams flitting across her eyeballs like notes in air guitar.

Two more blocks, another intersection. He put the car in neutral. With the handbrake set he could rev the engine, not loudly, but enough to make it purr. It was a habit he'd learned from a former girlfriend, one he had lived with before Mathilde; she had picked it up from her brother, and Dooley had spent the duration of their year-long arrangement trying to get her to leave the handbrake alone. But now he saw that it rather made sense, this precautionary measure, especially after he traded his snug and rusting Spitfire for the Moby Dick bulk of the Chrysler. Mathilde liked big cars. They reminded her of her childhood, she said. And after years of cramped legs, riding clutches, grinding gears, Dooley discovered their merits, not the least of which was all that trunk space. Excellent for transporting casebooks and files, with enough length and breadth for all his fishing tackle — a feature Mathilde had not, perhaps, anticipated. And so he had filed away his youthful rebelliousness, selling the Spitfire to an articling student. He kept his ponytail, however, ignoring the fact that it was scant and greying. It squiggled like a question mark when wet; in an affectionate mood, the two of them just out of the shower, Mathilde would corkscrew it round her finger. On those rare Saturdays when she rose early, before he made his getaway.

One more intersection, then the long stretch of sub-urban highway to the park. The hovering sun tinted the dove-grey dash a rosy ochre and, home free, Dooley stepped on the accelerator, felt the pleasant kickback of power as the engine responded. The clock said 6:09; another ten or fifteen minutes and the dog walkers would be out, their pesky animals disturbing the air and scaring the bass to the bottom.

For a half-mile or so he rode the bumper of a red Toyota. He kept thinking of his upcoming appearance in court to defend someone who happened to be an immi-grant on shoplifting charges. His specialty with Wegenstaff, Kinrade and Associates was immigration, which in a city this size meant, more often than not, deal-ing with petty crime. This was how he had met Mathilde — not as a defendant, but a witness in one of his legal aid cases. She was a cosmetician for a large department store, and she had testified when a thin young male who barely spoke English was brought in for stealing lipsticks. Not even quality stuff, Mathilde had said on the stand, brushing feathered blonde hair from the sides of her face. Dooley was amazed to learn she was a cosmetician, picturing cosmeticians as stout women in smocks, with deep painted lips and eyebrows and reeking of perfume. Not tall and willowy and hopelessly blonde, with the kind of skin that looked as though it would bruise if you touched it. She reminded him of a girl in an ad for baby shampoo, she was that pale and wispy, with eyes like a malamute, like the ice on a lake in February.

And so they had hooked up, he and beautiful Mathilde, she just twenty-four years old and brimming with hopes of ski trips to Austria and Caribbean cruises each March. To please her, Dooley stopped drinking beer and took up cooking and going discreetly to the bathroom whenever the urge hit to talk about a client. That had been the death of his last relationship, with the woman obsessed with braking: his uncontrollable need to discuss work.

That May, just one short month before, he and Mathilde had toasted the second anniversary of their living together; and though there was no talk of marriage, no cracks had yet begun to show in the affair. Although demands at the office had delayed any plans for vacation, and Mathilde was resisting his idea of their buying a house. They were still "shacked up" (as he joked to his colleagues) in his midtown apartment, the cramped upper flat of a pricey Victorian row house. Dooley had dreams now of moving somewhere out of the city, away from the traffic noise and sirens, somewhere out in the 'burbs, perhaps, somewhere close to nature. "Close to water, you mean," Mathilde would say, leaning over him on the sofa, scooting a strand of unruly hair behind his ear. She was so much taller than he, that at times she seemed to tower over him, especially while they were relaxing. Sitting with their feet up on his scarred glass coffee table and watching TV. When she leaned over him like that, those ice-blue eyes of hers tender yet sharp as taut fishing line, he couldn't help thinking of the heron he had once spotted perched among some other birds on a boulder in the pond. It was hunched and reedy as the villain in an old British movie. He couldn't help thinking of himself as a small, somewhat rotund and utterly undeserving duck. If anything, the apartment accentuated that: its windows high and arched like a cage, the mouldings chipped and in need of paint, floors and carpet worn with the exhaustion of too little space housing too much life.

At least that is how it seemed to him, in the beginning.

And then there was the simple lack of closet space — no room in the bedroom closet for his rod and tackle, with Mathilde's wardrobe in the way. One morning early in their cohabitation she had turned on him like a cat, when a fish hook snagged one of her skirts and pulled a thread like a drawstring through the slinky fabric. Her favourite skirt; she almost cried. He was gathering papers from his desk on the landing when he looked up and glimpsed tears, the ice of those eyes melting. "I'll replace it, Mathilde. I'm sorry," he told her over and over, with such sincerity he ended up fifteen minutes late for a meeting with a client, a Russian crewman who had jumped ship to remain in Canada.

He came home that evening with a new skirt, one that cost five times what the original had, and over dinner — a five-course Szechuan meal he painstakingly assembled — he proposed that they move.

"Oh, Dooley, give it a rest — forget it, would you? This morning? I was just PMS-sy; you mustn't take me seriously when I get like that. Listen—I mean, a house would be great. But, well, you know . . . I mean, when the time comes.. . ."

So Dooley shelved the idea, begging storage space in the basement. It was less than ideal, though, meaning he had to disturb the downstairs neighbour each time he wanted to go fishing, or leave his gear in the trunk.

And while Mathilde tended to be wishy-washy, at times she could be accusing. Like this morning. Lying cocooned in the expensive sheets she had chosen, her pale hair splayed against the yellow-flowered pillowslip, she had opened one eye, raised herself up on one thin elbow to click on the light. "Oh, for God's sake. Ow-oo-ow-oo-*ouch!* I've got this little tiny pain right in the middle of my — oh, Dooley, come back to bed!"

He knew, of course, that if he had he would have missed the best part of the day.

She flopped against the pillow, gazing at the moulding that circled the overhead fixture like an aureola. She stared as if fascinated by the greyish outlines of flies trapped in the shade. An idea sparked in Dooley's mind, a boyish curiosity about their suitability as bait.

"Dooley?" she interrupted. "What if nothing bites? I mean, I just don't understand."

But how to explain that it had nothing to do with bites or bagging anything?

He smiled and shrugged, even at that hour instinctively holding in his stomach to keep it from avalanching over the waistband of his baggy, khaki shorts.

"Well," she sighed, snuggling back down, alone, "if you *do* catch anything, don't you dare bring it home!"

He kept quiet, fumbling in the half dark with the laces of his hiking boots, and folding down the tops of his expensive, woolly socks.

"Um, Dooley?"

"Yeah —"

"Sweetie?"

"What, babe?" He hesitated. The names they had for each other often caused him embarrassment, even in the dim privacy of their bedroom. And he was impatient now to be going.

"Nice legs, Mr. Kinrade, legal counsel."

"Kiss off." Slouching to the bedside, he had leaned down and touched his lips to her throat, the faint, warm pulse below her ear. She had twisted away, shutting her eyes.

"Catch you later," she muttered, folding her arms over her chest.

Pulling into the parking lot, he glimpsed the pond through the trees: a dappling of light, mist threading the branches. The sky overhead was marbled pink. From somewhere beyond the woods he heard ducks squabbling, a faint splash and shearing of water. But nothing else, no other sound, except perhaps the remote tin-whistle cry of a loon. Good, he thought with satisfaction, with the same growling-bellied comfort one would feel tucking into a simple but decent lunch. The woods were still dark, and so quiet you could hear pine needles fall. The squish of his foot sinking into a spongy orange toadstool. Off the path, through the waist-high huckleberries he tramped, like a cartoon runaway with his rod slung jauntily over his shoulder, its hook dangling. As if these were his sole possessions, the rod, the hook, and the little cache of flies tucked inside his fanny pack. He always waited till he got outside to strap it on, the click of its clasp at the small of his back the last, abbreviated note in a volley of sounds: the whirr of unseen parts as the engine shut off, the trunk lid slamming shut, the scuff of his boots on gravel.

Somewhere in his imagination Mathilde yawned. The pond beckoned, mirror-grey and pocked with lily pads. It had been a dry summer so far, very dry, the waterline like a bathtub ring around the rocky perimeter, granite boulders like eggs dipped in tar, a black that reminded Dooley of licorice cigars, the kind with red, speckled ends that he and his friends "smoked" when they were kids.

Beside a beaver lodge banked like a washed-up mess of matchsticks, Dooley spotted his favourite fishing boulder. It was bleached granite, the size of a baby barn, and it jutted into the water. Under the climbing sun, the pond looked like a steaming skillet, shocks of purple azalea blooming along the edges. He thought of Mathilde, her limbs tangled in the sheets, still dead to the world, or perhaps, though not likely, propped against the pillows reading one of her magazines.

Dooley scaled the boulder, the stiff treads of his boots snagging its grainy slope. At the top he teetered a little while he gained his footing. Like his grandmother parking herself in slow motion into her nursing home chair, he crouched, then sat heavily, the ridge of rock driving a shockwave through his tailbone. He checked his Swiss Army watch, a birthday gift from Mathilde: 6:20. The place was still deserted, thank God. The only sounds were the faint hum of cars out on the road. No one had witnessed his geriatric imitation of a mountain goat. And there was nobody — yet — to shout out the message on the sign near the entrance: *Leave flora and fauna for others to enjoy.* As if he needed reminding. He was such a *good* person, Mathilde so often remarked, most notably during an argument. Such a go-by-the-rules type of guy, was how she had put it the last time, shoving past him to the bathroom mirror, pulling a monkey face as she rubbed on some sort of cream.

"Yeah? So? Without rules, what've you got? Anarchy!" As he spoke a memory flashed from law school, of some Marxist-Leninists marching outside the building, and how he had shouted, "Fuck you, make the poor pay, too!" The memory caused him to smirk, for Mathilde dropped the pot of face cream on the countertop, the two of them watching in silence as it ricocheted into the toilet. "Goddamn you!" she blurted, then broke into an embarrassed laugh as Dooley bent to retrieve it.

"I believe," she laughed, shaking with uncontrolled mirth like the tremors before a glacier lets go, "that rules are made to be broken."

And when it came to this place, this suburban pond and its secret stock of smallmouth bass, in spite of himself Dooley had to agree. In all likelihood it was a cesspool fed by faulty septic systems. Peering down, he watched for the shadows of catfish and carp nosing through the murky shallows like bumper cars. He could just make them out, if he stayed very still and concentrated hard on the steadiness of the boulder under his backside, and ignored the urge to close his eyes and savour the dampness lifting off the surface. Yet, despite his focus on the darting fish, he could not quite tune out Mathilde's voice: "Catch and release? Um. Duh? Am I missing something?"

Those were her exact words the first time they had come here together, not quite her idea of an enticing or enduring pastime, an early Sunday morning walk in the park. That day there had been kids fishing — catching weeds, he had figured, until the pair of them had chanced upon an angler balanced like a crane on what would become Dooley's rock, casting a line in the most perfect arc Dooley had ever witnessed. Then, wonder of wonders, watching through the bushes they saw the line jerk tight, the surface break, and the queer flapping birth of a fish into the air. With her arm looped through his, Dooley could feel Mathilde hold her breath under her sweater as the fellow reeled the fish in. It had to be two feet long, its sequined body flashing. She shook her head, watching the man unhook and toss it back. "The point, Dooley — is there one?"

Until then, Dooley had marvelled at how natural Mathilde's face always appeared, despite all the stuff she was constantly applying to it. But in that moment he realized how makeup made her look older; wary, if not cruel.

"That was a bass that guy just landed! I can't believe it. A smallmouth bass!" he couldn't help remarking, strolling back to the car.

She eyed him the way she did whenever he raised a point of law describing his day at the office. But Dooley hardly noticed; in his mind he was already knocking on the neighbour's door, asking for the key to the basement.

Mathilde had her good points, he told himself as he rose carefully to his feet. Centring his weight in his belly — the best means, he had heard, of keeping one's balance. Still, it was discomfiting to perch so high on such an irregular, unforgiving foothold. What if he slipped and fell in, banging his head on those rocks at the bottom? It would be hours before anyone found him, days perhaps. He imagined a stranger pulling him ashore, rooting through his wallet, dialling the police. The call being put through to one of the numbers on his card: who would find out first, his senior partner or his life partner? That was the term now — not "significant other," not "friend," or "lover," and definitely not "live-in" or "main squeeze," as they said on *Entertainment Tonight*.

He pictured Mathilde hanging up the phone, the grain of her cheek magnified by a tear.

Rooting himself to the rock, he attached the fly, an oversized Mickey Finn, and extended his rod, preparing to cast. A chorus of birdsong broke from a patch of cattails nearby, grounded by the distant rumble of a bus. Dooley pulled his arm up and back, the weight moving through his wrist as he brought it down, as measured and thoughtful as a senior taking her seat; and with a sharp intake of breath he listened to the whirr of the reel, felt the feathery snap of the line as it flew out and struck the surface.

It wasn't his best cast; the breeze caught the line and boomeranged it back towards shore, the fly dancing over the ripples those three or four seconds before the hook yanked it under. Eyes locked on the water, his mind wandered uneasily back to Mathilde. He imagined her in the bathroom splashing her face. In the kitchen, stirring whitener into the French roast he had hastily brewed, the last thing he'd done before collecting his gear. He imagined her going into the living room and putting on one of her pop CDs, slapping his easy-listening disk on the coffee table and leaving it there to gather dust.

Dooley was so engrossed in his thoughts that he almost missed the moment the hook caught and the line snagged taut. It was like being jolted awake. His heart in his throat, he started reeling, every ounce of effort flowing to his hands. Bracing his elbows against his sides, he pulled up and up on the rod — oh, yes, he had hooked a feisty one, he certainly had. A hefty one, too. The rod bowed until he feared it would snap — yes, yes — and then, almost like a slap in the face, the line jerked back.

Holding his breath, his tongue between his teeth, the high-wire whirr of the reel in his ears — a sound that reminded him, from childhood, of the hum of cicadas — Dooley watched his catch pop the surface with a sucking noise and skim toward him. It was almost in his hands before he realized what it was. His stomach kicked when he saw it had toes.

The foot looked as though it had been underwater for some time; it was bluish-black and bloated, the flesh shredded like stewed beef, a chunk nibbled from the heel. Gasping, Dooley dropped the rod and clambered backward off the rock, the pond tilting before him at a crazy angle. The smell was on his hands, a dead animal stink of muck and rotting meat. Skidding to the ground, he stumbled, his fall cushioned by peat moss. He glanced up at the rock, the rod dangling from it like a toothpick anchored by its awful quarry.

"Jesus, Mary, and Joseph," he crooned over and over, a mantra in time to the thud of his heart as he jogged the quarter-mile back to the Intrepid. He would have killed to see a jogger or a dog walker just then; but there wasn't a single other vehicle in the lot. It wasn't yet seven o'clock. Glancing back through the trees, that godawful stench in his sinuses, he remembered that the mist had only just risen. And that he had left his cellphone in his briefcase, miles away at home.

Dooley drove to the nearest RCMP detachment and described what he had found. By then he was able to crack a feeble joke or two: "No, it wasn't wearing a sock," and "No, not concrete, either." He answered the officers' questions but did not offer to return with them to the scene. "It's a really big rock with a rod and tackle on top. Trust me, you can't miss it." He told them he had something urgent at home: his partner would be worrying, wondering where the heck he had gotten to. She would think, honest to God, he had fallen in and drowned. "We'll be holding onto your gear," they explained, as if he were a dim-wit.

There wasn't a sound from the flat as he climbed the stairs a half-hour later, shaky and craving a shower. As he entered, he half expected Mathilde to call out from the bedroom, "What is that hum?" and start in: "I can tell you right now, I'm not eating it!"

The coffee maker was full, just as he had left it. In the living room, his Dire Straits CD was still in the machine. It was only eight-thirty; she must be sleeping in.

But as he tiptoed past the bathroom, Dooley noticed that the shower curtain looked wet. And not a sound came from the bedroom, no gentle snore or burble of traffic through the window. The window that Mathilde insisted on keeping wide open at all hours and in every season.

The bed was stripped; at first he figured she had made a trip to the laundromat, the one where you could sip espresso and surf the Internet while the clothes spun. But opening the closet, he saw that the basket was overflowing, its cascade all the more pronounced by the clang of empty hangers; and then he noticed the note:

Dear Dooley . . .

Dear Foot, it might as well have read.

In the kitchen, his hand trembled slightly as he raised the pot and poured coffee into a dirty mug. Its bitterness soothed him. As he sipped, he felt something slough off him, like something slippery and black from the bottom of his stomach. Her presence evaporating from his life as mysteriously, yet resolutely, as the fingers of a pianist lifting off the keys with the final note.

He would throw himself more into his work, that was all. He would cure himself, too, of that nervous and silly practice, his excessive use of the handbrake. He would make himself indispensable to policemen. He would take longer showers, perhaps even devote more time to personal grooming. This made him think of toenails: his own, and Mathilde's, painted a deep and jarring fuchsia — not, at least, the black or green of those of some others her age.

He would trim his hair, he decided, and get a bigger apartment. And he would fish wherever and whenever he damn well pleased, no matter what was swimming down there.

SECOND HEART

Michael Winter

THEY GO IN LADY SLIPPER ROAD AND HUNT WITH THE truck, cab lifting over potholes. Because the father's feet are bad. Splash in wheel wells and tilt and lean into each other. It's an intimate, unintentional touch of shoulders and knees. They haul off by a small pond the shape of a knife and pull back the red vinyl seat and dislodge two twelve-gauges and a Winchester pump and load up. The father instructs.

Only a bull, Gabe. If there's no antlers you leave it. If Junior's with you, let him shoot. I want this to be legal. You've got to be close to use a slug. Remember how far from the road you are. Don't go in miles. Keep the slugs separate. If you have a shell in the chamber, keep it breached. Your barrel needs bluing, Gabe.

A box of food from Mom all stacked to get the most out of a cardboard box — enough food for three days, really, but then Junior is with them.

Junior: Meat pie looks like it's going off.

Dad: Yeah, better eat it now. Sausage rolls, too.

You're right. That roast chicken, don't forget that.

It's Junior first as he has eyes that always see into the periphery. He sees black lifting wings near the pond. They eat the pie and walk toward it, Junior with the rifle, and the crows hop and lift and are annoyed. They haul away heavily from the bloated guts and front half of a rotting moose. The carved white hindquarters flayed.

Someone in a hurry.

The poachers had taken steaks, roasts. Carved them quick off the bone.

The father tries to turn the carcass with his boot but it rocks back into its own hollow. There is a scurry of beetles and the slow lift of maggots.

About a hundred pounds of meat.

There's disdain in his tight mouth.

Junior's eye now, roving, frozen on a cutover. Gabriel follows the eye to a mound of dead alders. But the branches are moving and, as he concentrates, the branches slowly separate into finer branches and antlers and the heads of three moose. There is only one with antlers. Junior already with the sights on him. The white bone of his cheek pressed to the stock. A shot hard on the air and the bull reels, his neck lowers and swings.

The cows.

Leave them, June.

Junior hesitates on the two cows. He sights, says quietly, Bang. He pivots the rifle three degrees, again says, Bang. But his trigger finger doesn't squeeze. He looks for the bull, but can't find it through the scope.

Is it down?

Dad: It went behind the rise. You got him now just leave him be.

The two cows stare straight at them, downwind, calm, lifting their noses. Now turn and trot quickly, shoulders full of alarm but almost haughty.

Junior is charging through high brush, rifle at the top of his arm, he sinks out of sight. There are three more shots. Gabe and his father make the rise and see Junior sizing up the strain and falter.

Dad: Don't go hitting the meat, June.

One cow on the knoll looking back. Hesitates.

Could get her, Dad.

You leave it.

The bull in deadfall.

Junior: They love to get into that. You shoot one in the open and he runs for the alders.

If you'd let him be.

Junior paces around the shoulders of the animal. He takes his time looking for a spot. Well that was quick, hey? He positions the muzzle of the rifle to the ear and fires and all four legs lift a little then strike the ground and relax. Junior pulls a knife from the back of his belt and tucks it under the throat. He rummages until a red gush pours over his hand.

The cow still lingers, nostrils flared, understanding all through her nostrils.

Remember the time when the eyes popped out, Dad? I was putting one through the ear, Gabe, and the force. Junior laughs. Held on by stringy things to the sockets.

Dad: That was ugly.

The cow twists and leaves.

They wait over the throat of the animal. They pass time by looking at the truck with its high cap on the woods road and the gap on the hill where the cow last was and understanding the lay of the woods road, which weaves through pulp mill cutover and heads to the highway. Then they begin the paunch. The father says, I wonder where that second cow got to. He knots a length of seat belt strap around one hoof and pulls it wide so the moose is splayed. He shanks this to a stump left by the Company. Junior punctures the belly and works the blade along, piercing a white membrane but not the stomach. A steam rises. His blade runs smoothly through the hide like a zipper. Blood sloshes into the cavity. Junior counts the ribs. Here, Dad.

They carve sideways between the third and fourth ribs. Hot blood leaks out the sides. They rock the moose to empty it of blood. The stomach, like an island in the blood, the yellow of chanterelles.

Junior approaches the head again. He cuts through backbone and slices the gullet. He works off the head and tosses it on some low bushes. One brown eye staring back at the body. If the eyes are closed it's still alive.

They return to the cavity, chopping through the boiled egg of sternum to pry open ribs. They coax the vast stomach down, slicing hitches that anchor it to bone.

Let's get him on his side more.

They roll out the guts. The father ties off the dark intestine with a rope and then separates the anus.

Where's the scrotum.

It's out already.

You should have left it on.

You don't want that, Dad.

You do want it, June.

I tossed it off in some bushes.

He wheels around, points with the knife.

Over there somewheres.

Gabriel checks the bushes and finds a strip of hide and the loose orange balls. He holds it up.

That's it.

He puts it up by the head.

Junior reaches into the chest, his shirt sleeves pushed up. The motion indicates he is cutting something — hoses. His hands appear with the heart. It is bigger than the platter of his hands. His silver watch is smeared in blood.

In my bag, he says.

Gabriel finds newsprint and Junior lays the heart on it beside the scrotum. He is careful with the heart. He wipes his hands front and back in the gorse and then up and down the thighs of his jeans.

I'm just going to see what's down there, Junior says.

Dad: You're not taking the rifle.

Junior: I emptied the mag. I just want to use the scope.

The father wipes out the ribcage with grass. Take a shotgun.

I'll take a shotgun too.

Well, make sure the action's —

It's empty. I'm waiting for some shotgun ammo, man. What, is it like we're in the army, are we rationing?

The father hands Junior shells, for birds.

They rest while Junior investigates the knoll. He is holding the rifle to look through the scope. Gabe and his father fall back onto the spring of alders. Look around. The father takes out a flask. He says, He's not supposed to do that.

It's dangerous.

There could be a cartridge. Don't do that, will you. Want some?

Gabriel takes the flask, but it's iced tea.

Good isn't it. I can't abide pop.

They have the pond to get round and then a bog to the road. From this angle the bog and pond are only long slivers of what they are. The wheelbarrow is in the truck. And Junior returns.

You see anything.

The mill got it all logged. Not a feather anywhere. You'll have to figure out a good route for us, Gabe.

Junior remembers the head and picks up his axe. He puts his foot on the nose to steady it. Then he hacks into the skull. When he swings, the butt of the axe nearly touches Gabriel's ear. The axe leaves blunt wedges in the skull, white showing through like coconut. They are sprayed with skull and brain.

Sorry about that. I should be doing this over here.

Junior drags the head by one antler to the side.

Gary wants the rack, he says.

The father waves Gabe back and they wait until the antlers are free. It's a small set of antlers, about eight points.

The bull last year was huge, hey Dad. Had four sprigs coming down over his eyes before the plate even started.

Junior puts his thumb to his cheek, fingers stretched out, to indicate the plate.

Gabriel finds a grown-over trail from a tree harvester, right to the road. He brings up the wheelbarrow. And watches his father carve out the lower jawbone. He has trouble getting through the hinge.

Let me at that, Dad.

Junior aims the axe at the hinge.

Watch the back teeth, June.

You want it here?

Just back.

When the jawbone is off, Junior wraps the scrotum around it and reserves it by the heart. So they won't lose any of it.

The scrotum to identify the sex. You keep that in the freezer for if the police come. The jawbone for Wildlife.

There is a blue dumpster outside the Irving gas station, a heap of skinned lower jawbones.

They saw off the legs above the talus and place them in a row. The father scalps a strip of hide off the spine. Gabe picks up the saw.

Junior: An axe is faster, Gabe.

Dad: Sawing is preferable.

Junior: You can tap an axe through and not splinter.

I like a clean cut, June.

They hold the front half while Gabriel saws. They pry open the quarters as the teeth descend, so the brace of the saw doesn't catch. Gabriel wipes the backbone clean to make sure he's straight. The bone is warm. He wouldn't have thought bone had heat.

Dad: That's a fine animal, June.

Yes, fine animal. Those cows were fine too.

Each quarter a hundred pounds, easy. The father takes out the silver tags.

Now Dad not yet.

It was supposed to be first thing.

Sure Dad we almost got this animal out.

Junior: We're tagging it.

He punctures a leg between tendon and bone.

Okay Dad. Thread em through but don't click em.

We've been through this, June.

Dad, it's only ten minutes to the truck.

And twenty to the highway and an hour to home. In my truck.

On my licence.

The father stands. Looks at Junior's chest. With your mother, he says. That licence is between you and your mother, and your mother won't have it.

Sure Mom don't need to know.

First thing she'll look for when it's hanging in the building. How come there's no tags?

We'll hang it over at Gary's.

June, I'm not having anything to do with Gary. If there's no tags involved, you're alone.

As Gabe and Junior carry out a quarter in the wheelbarrow, Junior: Dad, boy. A man of details.

In the dark of the truck, a beer each, sitting on the wheel wells. The moose quarters jiggling, the meat warm. They hold on for potholes. Junior says, If I come home I can work with Dad. I can make daybeds and baby cradles. I'll get Dad to show me. Because he needs a hand, Gabe. Like this truck. He didn't understand the gas consumption. It was eating gas. And I showed him the pollution gear. Marked all the hoses and gauges with chalk and we hauled out the works.

They are sitting in the back of the truck, the father driving. The night highway moving backwards, framed by the truck cap. A car passes and the tags glint on stiff legs above the tailgate.

Dad: We'll let that hang a week.
   Mom: It wasn't lying in its own blood again, was it?
   Junior: It was lying in someone else's blood.
   Junior slit its throat first thing.
   Because if it's like that, Al, I'm not having it.
   The meat's well cased.

The brothers share the bunk beds. Junior stretches his legs and makes the frame crack and fifteen years vanish. Teenage years of Junior home late, drunk, opening the window to pee and it splashes over the desk. Urine on the blankets.
   They watch headlights of cars arc over the bedroom wall.
   Christmas, Junior says. If I come home I'm coming home then. I'm getting a tree and really celebrating.
   What about Mom.
   Gabe, I'm having a tree. I know she calls that pagan. Well to say that is like me telling her to fuck off. It's Christ's birthday and I feel like enjoying it. And if she don't, then I'll live in Dad's building.
   A little later: Gabe, eventually I want to build a little cabin with twelve-volt lighting in Mount Moriah. I want to occupy the land and I don't care what happens. I'm gonna keep the land the way I like it and have a son who can take it over. I want you to do me a favour.
   Pause.
   Can you do me a favour?
   What.

A favour, boy.

Yes, what the fuck is it.

Look up the rules on building codes and old Newfoundland laws on occupying land. If you could get some books on it or show me where it's to.

Junior would get out of bed, leap down, and drive Gabriel with his leg. In the thighs and ribs. Gabriel vowed to hate him. I hate you. No you don't, he'd say. I'm your brother. You got to love me. You can't help it.

And Gabriel realizes this is true.

In the morning.

Junior: Gabe. Come on.

What's up.

We're getting Dad a load of wood.

He's got lots of wood.

Come on, Gabe. He's got bad feet. I got the saw in the truck. I got gas and oil. I even made you a little sandwich. Just half a load. We'll be done by one.

Is Dad going.

Dad can't be at that any more.

I'm too stiff.

Just you and me against some trees.

They take the truck and go in Lady Slipper Road again.

That deadfall stuff is rotten, June.

Oh Gabe's catching on.

Junior parks where they were parked before. And get out. It's cold and low light. Grey rolling nimbus. Junior takes an axe from behind the seat.

Okay.

Junior: You can't guess?

A sweat creeps into Gabe's armpits.

There's a moose in there.

Junior points the axehead to the knoll.

Man oh man they're long gone, June.

I'm not talking about the one that got away.

They walk past the bog and around the pond and the crows now at yesterday's remains. Dew wetting their jeans. The butchered head and swollen stomach of the bull. Four cut-off legs in a row. Four legs with no space between them. The respectful thing would be to give them space.

Gabriel follows Junior to the knoll. Where Junior had looked for birds through the scope. Gabe pans the clearcut. Then he sees the cow moose lying in full run in the clearing. Its throat cut.

Fuck, June.

Got her when I shot the bull. I was too quick for Dad. Aint she beautiful? Had to find her yesterday, cut her throat.

Jays are perched at the eyes.

You know what Dad does when he hits a moose, Gabe? He boils the kettle. That's what he wanted to do, boil a fucking kettle while that bull died. Moose sees you after him, he runs. If you hang back he'll lie down. He's hurt, see? Wouldn't have got this cow if we'd boiled a kettle now would we. Got to watch out for wardens, okay? Dad with his fucking tags. We coulda used them today.

A quarter rolls off his back.

Junior: The meat is some alive, hey?

We should've taken the barrow.

Dad would miss it. He'd say, you took the barrow for wood?

They take a quarter each, Gabriel carrying the lighter front quarters. Resting at the remains of yesterday's bull. Then all the way to the truck. At least there's the path the wheelbarrow made. But Gabriel stops with his second quarter.

Gabriel: I say we leave it.

Okay we leave it. But I'm getting the heart.

Junior jogs through the cutover, to the knoll, and down to cut the hoses that hold the heart to the lungs. He shuffles the heart under his arm and jogs back to Gabe.

Take the heart.

Junior hoists the last quarter over his shoulder. He strides hard for the truck.

Gabriel wraps the heart in newsprint and tucks it safe on a shelf in the cab. Junior rolls the quarter into the truck bed.

That's seventy-five dollars worth of meat, Gabe. Couldn't let that go to waste.

Okay, the deal is you drive and I sit in back with the moose. You're to rap on the rear window. If you see anything at all.

Gabe can spot Junior through the rear-view mirror. Junior with his hands ready under a quarter. And up on the hill where the road winds down is a white jeep. Gabriel slows. The jeep disappears into the green. Junior lifts the meat over the tailgate. He has to lift and throw the meat to the side so it makes the ditch. He lifts a second quarter and hurls this, too. Gabriel keeps it moving.

Junior pushes down the legs on the other two quarters and drapes himself over the moose.

The warden passes. Gabriel nods to him, but the warden's eye is on the back of the truck. The jeep halts in the side mirror. The warden is studying the truck. Gabriel tilts carefully through potholes. He wants the warden's brake light to wink out. He wills the red light to dampen and it does. The warden drives on. And Junior bangs on the window.

They back up and bring up the meat. The fresh bone and cut muscle stained in dirt. When they get to the highway Gabe pulls over. They cover the meat in a blue tarp and Junior gets in the passenger side. I'm beat.

There is a nasty cut across his wrist from a bone.

Couldn't get it all out in time. Dad got the fucking tailgate on. Tailgates are fucking useless.

Gabriel drives into town, up past the house, and down into Curling. Junior asleep against the door post.

Junior reaches over to press the horn. Stop here, Gabe. He jumps out and opens a screen door and disappears. He comes out with Gary. Gary is wearing a shirt that goes with a tuxedo.

Best to back her in, Gary says. Hi Gabe.

Gary puts on a red jacket and they take a quarter each down some stairs to a garage with a basketball hoop over the door and lay the quarters on spare tires. Junior returns for the last quarter.

Meat looks bloody. And dirty. Man, d'you drag it behind the truck? You run it down first?

Junior: It's good meat, Gary. Anyway look, let's settle up. I need some birch for the old man. Got a load of birch?

In the yard. Don't take my dry stuff.

We want lengths.

Lots of lengths.

Okay, Gabe. Move over.

Gary pulls down the door and doesn't even look at them. The yard next door. A heap of stacked eight-foot lengths of birch.

Junior: We're late but this is good wood.

They take more than a cord.

Gabriel packs for the airport. He has a cheap flight back. He's stacked frozen cuts from last year's moose in a cardboard box padded with newspaper. Another box has pickled onions, pickled beets, mustard pickles, and tomato chutney.

Mom: Got room for spuds?

In the basement, in a barrel of sawdust, are the blue potatoes. He fishes out about forty pounds.

When I was going grey, I told your dad he wouldn't love me anymore. He got upset. Which means he must've thought it a little. Anyway, I've written you all a little something and for your dad I've said, if we both make it, look for someone with red hair.

She says, I won't be hovering in heaven, as some people claim. And if you win an Academy Award don't say you know your mother's watching. I won't know anything until the resurrection.

Seeing him off.

Junior: You should buy my Dart, Gabe. Go back in the Dart. I'd have to take the stock car mirror off though. I want that. Parts are dirt cheap. Only problem is it's rear-wheel drive, so you got to have weight in back in winter on those hills in St. John's.

But he wants five hundred for it.

Dad, sizing up the wood. So, where'd you go for that?

Junior: In off Georgetown Road.

See Anthony?

No. No one in there.

Funny you didn't see Anthony. On a Sunday.

We were in a little further along hey, Gabe.

Gabriel nods.

It's good yellow birch. You didn't have trouble with the saw.

It cuts good.

I've found it losing power.

I was gonna tell you about that, Dad. I can have a look at it before I go.

I'd appreciate that, June.

And Gabriel shakes hands with Junior. Then hugs his mother, who's come down. It's good to have you, she says.

It's on their way to the airport. His father says, I hate to guess what you two were up to this morning.

Pause.

All I know is. That wood wasn't cut today. That wood's been seasoned.

But he helps Gabriel with the potatoes and shakes his hand at Departures. He hands him a piece of wood. Written on it along with today's date, is:

I, Al English, gave to my son Gabriel, a quantity of moose meat. Tags # 02946. He will be transporting said moose to St. John's, where he lives.

The woman swipes his feet. Steel toes, she says.

Are they?

She nods.

When the boxes go through she halts the conveyor. She scrutinizes the X-ray. You got moose steaks in there?

Yes.

Lucky you, she says. And hits the switch.

Gabriel sees his father waiting behind the glass; he mouths something, but Gabe can't understand it. He nods anyway. His father now in pantomime, and he sees it: the police coming to arrest Gabe. His father encouraging, and they both know he could have been angry.

Two weeks later, in a letter from his mother:

Your Dad said there was a smell coming from the back of the truck. He says he found a second heart.

CRUELTY

Libby Creelman

LILA IS SITTING ON HER HANDS ON THE EDGE OF THE dining room table while her parents dress upstairs. They rarely go out anymore, but when they do, her father needs the extra quiet time to shower and shave. Lila's mother doesn't want anyone coming up the stairs with a load of questions.

Lila can see the backyard, which is deep and narrow and suffers from a thick canopy of neighbouring trees so that even in summer it will be cold and overcast. Although snow remains now only in patches, it is not grass that has emerged but vibrant green moss.

The phone rings and Lila hears the clip-clop of her mother's shoes as she moves over the hardwood floor in the upstairs hallway.

"Yes, hello, this is Marian."

In the backyard stands a handsome wooden swing set Lila's father put together from a kit. A monument soaked with dampness but free of snow. He hammered his finger that day and Lila's mother ran up and down the stairs looking for Band-Aids. Her mother worries about splinters, but Lila hides them, along with the blisters, by making fists of her hands. Her mother distrusts the outdoors — in particular, backyards.

"Rick, it's for you."

There is the whispered shuffle of Lila's father in stocking feet as he travels to the phone.

"Careful, Rick, you'll slip. That won't be good for your back."

The maple trees are brown, and the tulip beds, the fence, the undersides of clouds. Her mother calls this another disappointing spring day in Newfoundland. Her mother is from Ontario and visits there sometimes alone, but comes back with a sad face and new clothes for everyone, saying there is no one left. A place called Kingston has become a foreign land.

Joy appears in the doorway. "Something's going on. Listen."

Joy is ten and does not sit on her hands while their parents dress. She sits in the kitchen and crayons.

Upstairs their mother says, her voice elevated and slightly frightened, 'You're only telling me this now?"

"No, Marian. *She* was only telling me this now. On the phone, just then."

"Is she crazy?"

"Marian." Their father sounds as though someone has applied glue to his tongue. Perhaps he is experimenting with a new painkiller. "Marian, it was an innocent, kind-hearted suggestion. She has children of her own, after all. But if the babysitter's here, let's forget it, shall we?"

"Has she already made their supper?"

"She didn't say. Is the babysitter here?"

"Do you hear the babysitter nattering away down-stairs?"

"Lila's on the table?"

"If she's already made their supper. Rick?"

"She didn't say." Her father comes to the head of the stairs. Lila sees his navy socks. "Lila, you can hop down now," he calls.

Joy puts her arms out and Lila slides down into them, then stands fanning her hands, imagining them attached to the ends of her arms like two pressed leaves. In a few years she'll wait in the kitchen with Joy while their parents dress upstairs, but she doesn't think about that now.

Upstairs, there is the hollow clip-clop of their mother and more slowly, the slithering hush of their father. The room where Lila and Joy wait is growing dark. The lights are not on and neither girl has the courage to touch their mother's antique lamps. The view onto Monkstown Road is aglow. In the sky above, dozens of crows are beating their way back from the dump to Kenmount Hill where they will spend the night. Lila knows this because her father has explained it to her. He has stood at this window and counted hundreds passing overhead.

"Girls?" He is there, almost ready, his hair combed back and still wet from his shower. He'll need help with his shoes. "How would you two like to head out with us tonight?"

"Yeah!" Joy says.

"Lila?"

Lila rushes her father, hugging him at the hips.

"Whoops," he says, taking her by the wrists and restraining her at arm's length, gently. "Careful of your old dad's back."

"I've called the babysitter, Rick," their mother shouts from upstairs. "But I'm having second thoughts.

Someone find your father's shoes, then everyone go wait for me in the car."

Lila's father puts a hand on Joy who, understanding the gesture, immediately pouts.

"Let your sister get them this time," he says. "It means a lot to her."

"Did anyone hear me?" their mother yells.

"Yes, Marian. Loud and clear."

"It's only common courtesy to make that acknowledgement, all of you."

His shoes wait side by side at the back door, smelling of leather, shoe polish, pain. As she lifts them, Lila has the desire to crawl inside one, down to the tips of the toes.

What Lila comes to understand on the drive over is that they are visiting a woman who works where their father did before he had to give up working. A woman with three sons, but no husband.

"I believe he went to California," their father explains.

"California? Good Lord."

"I believe he works as a mechanic at Disneyland. But don't quote me on that."

"Could he get us in free?" Joy asks. "Some kind of a deal?"

"Anything's possible."

"Oh, Rick, don't get their hopes up like that," their mother says with soft laughter. "Your father's talking out of the side of his mouth. Is this it?"

They park behind two cars in a single-lane driveway. On the left is a dusty turquoise house while on the right a chain-link fence travels past the cars and up a slight incline, bordering a backyard consisting mostly of mud. Lila moves forward in her seat and sees a single tree in the middle of the yard. In the bare arms of the tree hangs a boy.

"What's that?" her mother asks.

"Back of the brewery," Lila's father answers.

"Does it always stink this badly?"

"No idea. Come on, now."

A woman steps through the back door and waves.

"She's pretty," Joy says.

"I guess I was thinking a little more formal," their mother says.

Their father looks at the woman, then at his wife. The woman is wearing leggings and several layers of shirts, the outermost a man's red hunting jacket. His wife is wearing a new linen skirt and her boiled wool jacket.

"Don't sweat it," he says.

"I just wish I had known," Lila's mother says, swiftly removing her earrings and pocketing them — a sure sign that all is lost.

Lila watches her father's jaw clench, from irritation or pain or both. He wets his lips, as though to make a fresh start. "Come on, everybody out."

As they move toward the house a black dog charges around the side of it, barking and leaping over invisible barrels.

The woman, who has been smiling and shifting her weight from foot to foot, possibly to stay warm, stops and puts her hands on her hips and shouts, "How did Mackie get loose?" She seems to be addressing the boy in the tree. As though the black dog understands this it immediately heads that way, its tail batting the air unrhythmically. A German Shepherd rises from the dirt at the base of the tree and yanks hard against the rope at its neck. The two dogs grapple briefly, and the black dog is off again.

"Brrr," the woman says, hugging herself as Lila and her family approach. "So you brought the kids. Excellent. Watch out for Mackie. Down, boy!" She turns and hollers, "Alfred!"

"I'm stuck. I can't get down," the boy in the tree answers. He does not shout or raise his voice yet speaks with such forceful clarity he could be standing at Lila's ear.

"What a liar he is," the woman tells Lila and Joy. She seems to find this funny. "Alfred's after living in that tree. Mackie! Down, boy."

The dog is avoiding the woman. Lila's father reaches for its tail, misses, and lurches awkwardly. He puts his hand on his lower back and his family stops breathing.

"Now you've done it, Rick," their mother says. "Do you want to go home?"

"Of course not. We only just got here." Then he winks at the woman and jokes, "I'm used to living with phenomenal pain."

"Sure?" the woman asks, alarmed. Turning swiftly she seizes the dog by its neck and twists one of its ears until it slides onto its haunches at her feet and whimpers, its tail a submissive thud-thud on the wet ground. "Oh, now, will you look at your paws. Down, boy. Get down out of that!" She straightens partway, still holding the dog, and smiles. "How's it going, Marian?"

"I can't complain."

"Come on in. It's freezing out here."

"Two dogs," Lila's mother says loudly. "That's two more than I could handle."

"Don't be talking! It wasn't my idea." The woman opens the door with one hand and drags the sitting dog over the steps with her other, then puts her foot on its rear and shoves it the last distance. Lila's father and mother follow. Joy moves with her mother as though connected by a rope.

Lila doesn't budge and they disappear inside without her. She turns and stands a long time watching the boy in the tree as he climbs up one side and down the other and then back into the centre. Suspended in the branches around him are various items: a beef bucket swinging by a yellow rope, a checkered cloth bag, torn ribbons, Sobeys bags, and partially deflated balloons. He's wearing a jean jacket over a grey sweatshirt with the hood snug on his head.

"Can you climb a tree or what?" he finally asks.

Lila's been waiting for this. Although she has never climbed a tree in her life and she's wearing a dress and she's cold, she runs over to the tree. The German Shepherd rises like a wave.

"That thing won't hurt you. She's a big baby. Give her a pet. That's what I'd do."

"What grade are you in?" Lila asks, hanging back.

"Grade three. I hates it."

"I'm in grade two."

"Sure, you don't look old enough for preschool."

Lila has heard this before. She won't look at the boy now. She studies the dog digging at the ground with a single paw and panting so frantically its tongue skims the ground. Suddenly it barks and Lila jumps back and falls. She looks at her dress.

"Hey, don't cry," the boy says, scrambling down through the branches. He swings from the bottom branch and lands gracefully on bent knees, his arms extended before him. He lowers his arms as his body straightens, then bows so slightly Lila nearly misses it. "Don't go in."

But Lila has no intention of going in. The first thing she notices about him when he squats beside her is the space between his two front teeth, which are new and not as white as the others. She says, "It's just my dress is dirty, is all. My mother will kill me."

The boy looks away down the yard, squinting at the back of the brewery — a mustard-coloured building. He turns back and looks again at Lila's dress as though he can't quite make up his mind about it.

"What's your name anyway?"

"Lila."

"Wanna come up in my tree?"

Lila points at the German Shepherd. Alfred nods and stands, takes a few steps toward the dog, then charges it, leaping onto its back and pinning himself to its neck. It whines and tosses its head.

"Hurry," Alfred urges, though his voice is calm, almost gentle. "I can't be holding Girlie forever."

She gets to the tree and stops, unable to reach the bottom branch.

"See the nails?" Alfred says. "Use 'em as steps."

"Nails?"

"In the bark there."

Lila has never touched a nail. She remembers her father hammering his hand, the search for a Band-Aid. Both her parents had been shouting.

"Look at the bark," he says, still patient. "Jesus, Girlie, you're gross. Give it up."

Lila glances at Alfred flat on his back in the muck with the dog planted over him lapping his face. Hot gratitude rushes through her. She puts a foot on a bent nail lodged in the bark. When both feet have left the earth and she's reached the bottom branch, she hears him say, "There you go," and knows she'll be unhappy now for a long time because she was not born into this family.

He swings back up into the tree and joins her. "We're too low," he says. "Them piranhas can still get at us."

She follows him up to an opening where the bark is well scarred and he can reach his things. He takes a knife out of the beef bucket and scratches something into the branch between his legs, then offers Lila use of it. She shakes her head and he tosses the knife back into the bucket, saying, "Maybe another day, then."

He lets go with both his hands and leans back, his legs grasping the branch like hands. She wants to shout. Or touch him. His hood slips off and jacket falls open. She sees his torso tighten and his expression gain years as he grabs at the checkered cloth bag hanging from a branch behind him.

"My music bag," he explains, sitting forward again. Inside the bag is a Sobeys bag and inside that several Oh! Henry bars. "I'm the only kid I knows still has Halloween candy."

She says, "My mother won't let me go trick-or-treating." He gives her a short, satisfied nod and she knows she has said the right thing.

Cars are pulling up and people getting out and coming up to the house. Lila watches her own car become blocked in. The people wave at Alfred and Lila in the tree as they pass, but Alfred ignores them. "Jerks," he mumbles, his mouth full of candy bar. He's fishing around inside his pants, scratching himself and grimacing. He pushes his pants down and handles a small nubby object that seems to be irritating him. He slaps it.

He looks at her and smiles. "Just my old penis breath." He shoves it back into his pants, then slaps his zipper.

"Who were all those people?" Lila asks.

"Jerks. Have you ever been to Disneyland?"

She grins. "I know."

"What do you know?" He sounds cross.

"Your father has a job there."

"And that I visits there whenever I wants?"

She's hoping he'll invite her. She's hoping so hard, she doesn't notice him lean over and take hold of a strand of her hair. He yanks it out.

"Did that hurt?" he asks.

"No."

"It was hanging in your face."

"I wonder if it's time for supper?" she whispers.

"Sure, could be finished by now. Were you expecting someone to call you in? Gotta just go. Hold it." He raises a hand and pauses, waiting until satisfied he has her full attention. "Girlie's not asleep yet, I wouldn't make no move. You got another loose hair. Did that hurt?"

"No."

The next Saturday Lila is playing in her bedroom when her mother comes in and says, "That was Alfred's mother on the phone. Remember the little boy you got so dirty with? He wants you to visit him this afternoon." Her mother scrunches up her face. "That's not really something you want to do, is it?"

Lila has been thinking about Alfred and his tree all week. "Oh, Mommy, yes, please!"

"Let her make up her own mind, Marian," Lila's father says from somewhere.

Her mother frowns. "All right. But I'm going to put out pants and a wool sweater for you. Their house was freezing. And wet."

"Why was it wet?" Lila asks.

"Shame you never uttered more than two sentences, Marian," Lila's father calls.

"Because she had just washed the floor! There were puddles, in fact. I took off my shoes to be polite and then my feet got wet and I froze. I don't think they had the heat on, quite frankly."

"Marian."

"Yeah, yeah, yeah. I'm just explaining why she needs to dress warmly. And don't remove your shoes inside their house."

"We'll probably play outside," Lila says carefully.

"No climbing trees," her father says.

"Where are you, Rick?"

"I'm resting my back."

"Of course no climbing trees, Lila; that goes without saying. Children are forever falling out of trees and breaking their arms."

Her mother walks to the doorway and looks down the hall. "Is that comfortable?" she asks him.

"Nothing's comfortable."

*

That afternoon while Lila is at Alfred's, her father checks himself into the Health Sciences. He drives over himself without change for the meter or telling anyone, then calls just before supper, medicated and humble.

Lila's mother drops the supper plates before the girls, hurls the pots and pans into the sink, the leftovers into the refrigerator. Everything she touches she seems to hate. "Are you mad at me?" Joy whines.

"No, treasure. Your father. He's set on doing everything his own way. Again. Now I'm going over to that hospital and we'll have two cars collecting tickets. I mean, why didn't he just ask me for a lift?"

"You're going to the hospital?" Joy asks.

"Well, I think I better. They might operate." For a moment her voice lightens, as though she's amused by the idea of not rushing to her husband's side. "Although, frankly, this place. The medical care. It takes forever to get anything done. I mean, a simple X-ray?"

Lila puts a finger into each of her ears. But she can still hear the crying Joy will begin any moment.

"I could have dropped him off this afternoon then picked you up at that boy's house," she says to Lila. "It was right on the way." She slams the refrigerator door and on top of it the ceramic bowl of apples bounces towards the edge. "No, he has to do everything his own way. Now settle down, both of you."

The phone rings. It's sitting right there in the middle of the table and they all jump. Joy and her mother both reach for it, but Joy is quicker.

"Just give it to me," their mother hisses.

Joy hands the phone to her mother, who immediately tries to interrupt. "If I could just—" she begins, then stops, her head thrust forward with the air of someone struggling with the incomprehensible. She looks so annoyed Lila thinks she might bite the receiver. "Sometime, perhaps. Can I get back to you on this?" She hangs up and looks at Lila curiously. "So, you know about this? You want to have a sleepover at that boy's house? That woman is really getting on my nerves. From the moment your father tried to collar that mutt of hers he's been paying for it. Of course they'll never operate. Not after three operations already. Nobody'll touch him."

Alfred has long lashes and black hair that his mother trims with the scissors on her jackknife. She also uses the jackknife to open cans of tuna fish and tomato soup. Lila is fascinated by the speed with which her hand circles the can.

Today Alfred showed her his rocks. He keeps them on a wooden shelf on his bedroom wall. Lila didn't think much of the collection at first, the rocks were so dirty and crumbling. She would have expected a fleck or two of silver or gold — this being Alfred, who has been to Disneyland. The game they played with the rocks involved putting a bunch in their socks and underwear and down the backs of their shirts, then going out into the tree. Alfred took a while selecting hers.

As they approached the tree, Alfred tackled Girlie, again urging Lila to hurry. She scrambled up through the branches despite the rocks under her feet and between her legs, so thrilled when Alfred praised her that it was easy to make peace with her pain. As it was later, when he plucked out her hair or took her hand and bent it forward at the wrist until the tips of her cold pink fingers brushed her coat sleeve.

"Does this hurt?"

"No."

"Does this?"

"No."

"You got a gift there, girl."

She looked away, afraid he'd see her happiness. It came to her naturally, this gift.

Her father returned from the hospital unopened, grey and muted, with a new prescription that made him feel so stupid he tossed it out within a day.

Lila's mother's enthusiasm for housework immediately began to wane; she roamed the house glum and short-tempered until at last she decided to make a visit back to Ontario.

She stood at the door with her bags and said, "I've just got to get out of here, Rick."

"I understand."

"I'm not trying to punish you."

"Have a good time, now. Enjoy yourself."

"I don't know why I'm going. I can't relate to any of those people anymore."

"Go on. Don't worry about a thing."

"Yeah, yeah, yeah. Oh, look at your poor daughter."

Joy was coming down the hallway, sobbing.

"I'm counting on you and Lila to help your father. Don't hang off me, treasure."

Lila was sitting at the top of the stairs. She wouldn't come down. It was always a little scary when their mother left, shucking her role as though the antique lamps and polished floors, the sweet-smelling sheets and nicely dressed daughters, had never meant anything to her.

Although the last thing in the world they did was help their father. He shuffled around the house in his pyjamas, ordered Chinese food and pizzas, and let the house get turned upside down. It was understood that their mother expected to come home to a frenzy of domestic chores.

With her mother away, Lila began to visit Alfred more often. She rarely saw his brothers, but his mother would be there, the cordless tucked under an ear as she patrolled the house, busy at some new project, the most recent being the washing of all the windows with vinegar and newspapers. She'd laugh and nod and carry on, and gradually the house bloomed with an acidic odour that clung to Lila's clothes long after she was home again, a reminder of that foreign world that was her secret.

Alfred's mother had relaxed rules about food, and without argument allowed them to carry off whole bags of Mr. Christie's Favourites or Raspberry Temptations. Perched beside Alfred in the tree, Lila could only eat two or three — the smell of the brewery so close it seemed to route its way through her own bloodstream and slowly escape her lungs — but Alfred could always finish the bag. Occasionally he dropped one onto Girlie, who would be moving around on her belly in the muck below, her yellow eyes turned up to them with longing.

"You and me," Alfred said one day, removing a rusty wire dog brush from his jean jacket. "We could get married."

"Soon?" She held her breath.

"No. What are you saying?" He pinched her. "When we're grown up. Pinky swear?"

He offered her his little finger, crooked like the letter C, and she put her own into it.

That night, Lila dreamed that she and Alfred had climbed high into his tree. Overhead, the crows were going home to roost, calling out in unnatural voices that reminded her of her father's electric razor. The sound racked the tree, convulsing the branches and scaring Lila, so Alfred set to wrapping her in bedclothes that smelled of flat Coke and mown grass but which were as soft as anything and radiated heat. She had been so cold before. Then he tied his rope around her waist and lowered her, face first, toward the earth.

She dropped over Girlie, who whined, the sound echoing off the back of the brewery, which had moved so near the tree Lila could see where the last coat of paint did not quite cover the first. Then Girlie opened her mouth and without warning her face was transformed into the face of Lila's father, staring up at her with shining yellow eyes.

It had been sunny all day. In fact, it had been sunny two days running and in the morning Lila's mother had opened a window to admire the daffodils that had emerged, slightly crooked, in the backyard. She stood there, inhaling deeply, bestowing upon this view such a rare generous smile that everyone felt they deserved to be happy. After that she spent several hours going up and down the stairs, humming "I'll Be Home for

Christmas," cleaning house, and fetching things for Lila's father who moved from room to room, floor to floor, looking for comfort.

Lila had been to Alfred's in the morning. When she got home she changed into her nightgown and got into bed and lay facing the ceiling, her hands tucked fast beneath the small of her back. Her body hurt from the rocks and the dog brush. Her scalp seemed to belong to someone else.

"Lila?" Her mother came into her room carrying an armload of dirty laundry. "Did they give you lunch?"

Lila nodded. "She can make six sandwiches out of one can of tuna fish."

"Like I'm surprised. Why are you in bed?" Her mother moved across the room, gathering up Lila's clothes at great speed. After a while she let everything drop back to the floor except for Lila's underwear, which she shook timidly, and together Lila and her mother watched the broken rocks fall to the carpet.

She had to call Lila's father several times, and when he appeared he looked sad and his body thoroughly askew. Lila's mother showed him the underwear, and at once the two of them began glancing at each other, then back at the underwear, like a couple of hens, until he took it in his hands and looked as though he might lift it to his nose, but Lila's mother said sharply, "Rick!" and he stopped.

Lila watched her parents. It was like stepping into another world to see the skill with which they could suddenly communicate.

"Dear," her father began casually, but Lila wasn't fooled. "Who took your clothes off?"

"No one did."

"You did?"

"No."

"Treasure, they have dirt in them."

"I put rocks in them. And in my socks. And down the back of my blouse. I did it."

"Could you tell us why?"

"It's Alfred's game. He taught me."

"Just Alfred?"

"Yes."

"But why did you put rocks in your underwear?"

"To protect me."

"From what?"

"Alfred, see, he's worried about piranhas. But I liked the way it felt. I liked the pain."

Her father stepped back to rest against the wall. Her mother folded up the underwear. Both seemed to have become less interested, and Lila was in agony that they would leave the room. They didn't understand.

"Pain," her father said. "Christ almighty. Why would anyone want pain?"

"I do. I want to live with it. It's like . . ." She lowered her voice, wanting only her father to hear. "It's like I want to marry it."

"What are you saying?"

"That's all you were doing?" her mother said. "Putting rocks in your underwear? This is just a little too peculiar for me, Rick. I don't want her over there."

"Neither do I."

"I hope you realize this is your fault."

"Give me a break, woman."

"But, Daddy, you live with pain."

"Not by choice, I sure as hell don't."

She had expected admiration, reward, a tight hug. "But, Daddy—"

"I didn't choose this life! Do you understand me?" He was angry. When he was angry, he hurt more. "Does everyone understand me?" he shouted.

Although her father rarely raised his voice, Lila was not surprised, but it exacerbated her cuts and bruises so that her skin seemed to leap from her bones. She closed her eyes. She thought of asking them to leave if they couldn't be quiet.

"You could try another doctor," her mother said, angry in her own way, which was more knife-like and brittle. "You could try another province. Or maybe you like hanging around this house year after year, making us all miserable with your bellyaching."

"You just have no idea, do you?" As he spoke he travelled across the room, gritting his teeth because he was having such a bad day, and shoved Lila's mother against the bedroom wall.

Lila's voice was raspy, as though her throat had been injured in some way, but her shouting served to draw her father off her mother and back to her. As he came toward her, his misery and rage shining, Lila realized that this was the father she had been a long time expecting: the man inside the man who without complaint stooped crookedly at the back door to remove his shoes, rose slowly from a bed, or cleared the corner in the upstairs hall in his stocking feet just seconds ahead of disaster.

IDENTIFYING THE MUSES

George Elliott Clarke

And how beautiful, beautiful, beautiful—
—Lowry

IT'S A HUMAN TENDENCY WE DETECTIVES UNDERSTAND, this habit people have of collecting things they think "meaningful." Usually, it's records, or books, or dolls, or coins, or stamps. Fairly harmless, really. Unless the compulsion explodes into violent affronts to other collectors. (I've seen it happen: fans turn fanatic and horrible. If you ask me, flea markets need cops worse than stadiums.) Eccentric collectors may go for tropical parrots, or weird animals, like the most ferocious kinds of inbred pythons. Sometimes, people'll get odd — well, actually, pretty often, and their tastes'll run to mosquitoes, or catalogue models, or rodents, or lichens, or crutches, or, in one case, snow (the nut had a house full of refrigerators, and he even kept "yellow" snow as a specimen; we suspect he'd sugar it and dish it to neighbours' kids as ice cream in the summer, with never a hint of complaint). If you read newspapers, you already know that felons like to compile body parts, or seduce and kidnap children, or, more rarely, stack up corpses in cellars, and, naturally, all over mom-and-pop suburbia, and in more offices and temples than one would like to imagine, exist incredible caches of crud. (Don't think cops are prudes; we're not. We understand: in the backs of many "healthy" minds, there must needs be a private, secret space where unmentionables can be dumped.) To be explicit, for every proud display of Barbie dolls or riding whips or Batman comics, there's likely tucked away under a bed or in a closet, some sicko, psycho detritus: soiled lingerie, or Nazi junk, or extremely messy videos that provoke even cold-blooded morticians to puke. (I've seen a poor-quality film of a tied-up pooch, being repeatedly stabbed, its left ear bitten off, blood scattering everywhere, while some sable-hooded man sodomized its rear. Excuse me for saying it, but there's no point jailing vomit like that; you just shoot him, cleanly, and end civilization's suffering.)

Don't think artists are immune to such toxins! In my experience, there's no difference between those who paint crimes and those who commit 'em. Nope, especially the poets. Remember that detective wanna-be, Poe, and his unhealthy lust for his child-cousin? Rimbaud used to run guns and trade Negro slaves and he committed wicked, vile sins with Verlaine. Syphilitic, Baudelaire set precedents for evil imaginations. Whitman was potentially treasonous, but Pound defiantly was. (Why wasn't he hanged?) Byron, Shelley, all the Romantic sods, wouldn't pay their bills and left dead women — suicides — and dead girls — incested or neglected children — in their slimy, but flower-strewn, paths. Louis Carroll — a.k.a. Charles Dodgson — was a kiddy porn king and maybe child molester. That jerk,

William Burroughs, iced his wife by aiming his pistol too low at the apple she'd supposedly balanced on her head in some bastard's game of "William Tell." (It happened in Mexico, so Burroughs dodged a murder rap. Life is tequila there.) My advice? Steer clear of writers! A bunch of alcoholic malcontents, abusers of themselves and innocence, "no-incomepoops," the most ungodly, irreligious, impious, bitter, and unpatriotic sots and dolts. Usually, they can't even spell, and their grammar's as bad as their odours, their intentions, and their morals. Abominable abominations, all. *All.*

Look at this diary we've turned up. Diaries are beautiful evidence because they expose the brain's erupting, naked chaos. We have this case. You know about it. They're far too common, though always attention-getters. A so-called poet, with a milky, glass eye (or "orb": can you believe such infantile English?), an icky smell, and unkempt and bankrupt clothes, stole into the rectory of Paradise Baptist Church, surprised the twenty-nine-year-old minister's wife and mother of two, Louisa Guilfoyle (an almost Pre-Raphaelite beaut, really), at her baking, tied her up with her own stockings, forced her to satisfy his bestial wants, including assaulting her while her infant daughter howled in the crib beside the marital bed. Luckily, he abandoned his mayhem at that, though we also see evidence — matches and gas — that he tried to set the house and the church afire. (He's from Burnt Church, which may be the motive, you know, psychological.) Anyway, we searched his ratty, musty, cockroach room after we trapped him in a K-Mart (the only place would-be poets can ever afford to shop), and we found — Chrissakes! — standard garbage: a copy of

Lolita (well-thumbed), empty bottles of miasmic liqueurs (mead, ouzo, grappa, schnapps), stolen fountain pens (all dry), rotting journals, pricey books with artsy nudes (women draped with fishnets or tinsel). And guilt-proving things: a framed photo of Guilfoyle (so he'd been eyeing her for a while; not unusual in such cases) and this "Ready Diary." Here I found his "Muses." You know, criminals — like all artists — have muses. Here it is — but it's not for quotation, you understand:

"They haunt the Sea of Literature, that lecher's Sargasso, enjoying their immoral immortality, as beautiful as Nova Scotia girls generally are, kilted, svelte, and cunning. Lolling on cliffs, sandbars, and indecently erect and protruding stones, they comb their long hair and moan their names, synonymous with ominous love. There is Spenser's Duessa, half-naked, brilliant in crimson and purple, slinking wine into her mouth; Nabokov's Lolita, sucking on a lollipop and, legs akimbo dexterously wide, flashing her thong underwear; Jonson's common tramp, anorexic Celia, undoing her stays; Herrick's casual, well-practised strumpet, Julia, lounging amid the liquefaction of her clothes; Catullus's unique harlot, Lesbia, licking suspicious, white flecks from her thin, chapped lips; Flaubert's blushing, bourgeois adulteress, Emma, fingering a scrofulous, French novel; Sade's delicious Juliet, stripped and tied face-down to a bed; Shakespeare's jewelled trull, Cleopatra, slouching lasciviously on her burnished throne; Réage's perverse martyr, O, inviting, with her too-black hair and cleft red lips, cruel, violent pleasures; Cohen's dirty, St. Lawrence River siren, Suzanne, wringing tears from her tattered bra and welfare undies; Garcia Marquez's unfortunate teen-slut, Erendira, wearing only stiletto-heeled pumps, sprawling funkily on a tired rug; Cleland's tavern trollop, exploiting her name with her cheery, just-waxed ass; Nin's voluptuous "Queen of the Whores," Bijou, writhing in an agony of desire, honey streaming down her vanilla legs; Richardson's humiliated Clarissa, twisting her spunked-on hips that beg a thousand whips; Zola's dramatic slut, Nana, cavorting cunningly in a diaphanous gown (too light for Nova Scotia and too sheer for me); Lawrence's cuckolding bitch, Constance, slumming in the tulgey woods; Chaucer's lewd bawd, the Wife of Bath, tugging off her scarlet stockings; and Hawthorne's classic debauchee, the Puritan adulteress, Hester, squeezing her luscious dugs. The entire marine bordello betrays liquor of generation: Impatient as breakers and twice as wet. Craven, its members crave . . . They are lovers authors don't got to fight with to get their panties off. (Intaglioed in the blue cardstock cover of Bulliet's *The Courtezan Olympia* is a supine, sumptuous, zaftig nude, her black-ink breasts glaring — like eyes, alley-cat eyes — at me . . . In the rubricated pages of *My Secret Garden,* a stained, watercolour illustration reads, 'The walls of her ***** clasped my hammer vigorously. Her **** was like she was: fresh, dewy, and sultrily tight.' There's *lust* in it — what's left over from *lustre.*)

"Black. This province of dirty — and dirtying — words. Decay. Confusions of *Coriolanus* with *cunnilingus* (and *anus*), *paramours* with *parasites.* Because of whinnying blood in coke-snorting veins and coke-oven hearts. So dolls learn to scissor and vise their legs, to paint Cleopatra faces onto Desdemona bodies. White women who are practically white. In church, a room full of hanged birds. Whipped Cream and Black Ass Blues."

There's page after page of this bilge, but you can't divulge any of it. Nope, you can't say a word. This poet's offal is a dung-heap. Once again, we see here the failure of a poetaster to rise above self-flagellation. Need I point out his flawed tenure as a priest (alleged buggery), his rancid room (with actual maggots squirming inside a half-broken light-bulb), his messed-up taxes, his extremely debilitating stench, his bank that laughs in his face when it isn't suing him for fraud, the charge of fraud that he never escapes once some obscure rag pub-lishes his — laugh — verse, his atrophied prick small enough to go through the eye of a needle, his lick-spittle manners, his waspish criticisms of superior writers, his niggerish — excuse me — language full of smashing and destroying sounds, like a slaughterhouse? He's the sort of artist-con who'd put stained glass windows in a tarpaper shack and call it lovely. He may be black, really black, but he's not a poet, a real poet. I'm glad he's in the clink. Some punk should bust his hands now so he can't ink any more of his noxious rubbish that's only obscure when it's not plagiarized.

Really, it's no excuse to say that this hell is Halifax, where sewers empty effluent straight into the Atlantic, and prostitutes, milling, yawning, parade around the Legislature as soon as the sun goes down. (You've heard the awful joke about whores being called "parliaments" because "they seat many members"?) We can't, as a civi-lization, set aside whole populations for vice, just because of their location. As a detective, I'm biased, of course. But I do think it's our job — hell, it's our fate —

to protect beauty, and so, I don't mind, I don't mind locking up drunks on the Commons, vicious ass-peddlers on Spring Garden Road, frat-boy rapists down by the Rotary. May I say that we police are the only loyal *artistes?*

I'm swearing you to secrecy. Why? Well, I may be a detective, but, like you, I am sensitive to the taste and touch of what constitutes Man, for I am of that breed myself. Yes, my secret is, really, *I am like you.*

BLAMELESS

Peter Norman

QUEENSLAND BEACH WAS HOPPING. A BUNCH OF GUYS were in from Halifax with girls and loud cars. But the girls were off-limits. Their boyfriends prowled around, staring down the locals like we were good as ground meat. Jason went right up to one blonde and touched her hair. A guy was there in seconds, hustling her away and jawing at Jason, who just smiled and shrugged. Robert and I watched it happen, sitting silent on our log.

"I like a beer," Robert said. He had the bottle nestled against his cheek, rolling it over the stubble. As far as I could tell, he hadn't taken a sip.

"Drink up," I said. My pulse was pounding under my cheeks. It was my idea, the beer. Jason brought it, but I had the notion to try it out on Robert. See what happened. Have a laugh or two.

I was bored those days. Hot and bored. Six days a week at Fred's Fishing Shack, mending nets and selling bait and renting out the dinghy to tourists. Fred was there every morning at six when me and Jason arrived. He'd look up from his paperwork. "Plenty to do, boys. Plenty to do."

Maybe there was, but the time stretched and stretched like an elastic between your finger and thumb.

You'd wait for it to snap and fly off, for something to happen. But nothing ever did.

Halfway through his beer, Robert started doling out the laughs I'd hoped for. He tried to balance on the log standing on one leg. But he kept falling off. He'd shake the sand from his hair and try again. A few guys came over and watched, sipping their drinks and snickering. Craig McMurphy joined the crowd. He had slimy hair like wet seaweed. "Who is this guy?" he said.

"His name's Robert," I answered. "You know Fred? Runs the Shack? That's his son."

"How come I never seen him at school?" said Craig.

"Special needs. Goes some place up north."

One of the Halifax guys stepped forward. "Who gave that kid beer?" he said. "Did he ask for it, or what?"

"He likes beer," I mumbled. "He said so."

The guy looked up at Robert. Studied him. "I don't know," he said. "Doesn't seem right. How do you know he can handle his beer?"

"We don't," said Craig, with a little high-pitched laugh. "That's the beauty."

"So who the hell gave him the beer, then?"

Craig pointed at me.

The guy turned square to me; I shrank away. Robert tumbled off the log again.

"Hell's your problem, man?" said the guy. "This ain't right."

"It's harmless," I said. "Just some laughs, is all."

The guy shoved me and I stumbled back, kicking up sand.

"Is there a problem?" Jason had arrived. He tapped the Halifax guy's shoulder. "I'm talking to you, fuckwad. You got a problem with my buddy?"

The guy turned around. "He's feeding liquor to a goddam retard."

"And you have a problem?"

"Yeah. It ain't right."

They were face to face. Jason was shorter, but he stretched up on his tiptoes, sticking out his jaw. "Robert's my friend. He wants to drink, he drinks."

"You're fucked up, man. You got no sense."

"Mind your fucking business," boomed Jason. Then he lunged.

Me and Jason first met Robert at the Shack. He came in one afternoon around closing time. He looked our age, but big-boned and muscular, with stubble — I couldn't grow stubble; I'd been trying for a month. But Robert's eyes were what I noticed right away. They looked younger than the rest of him, large and unblinking. Soft blue.

Fred introduced us. He spoke real quiet, like he was embarrassed, or maybe just being gentle.

"Boys, this is Robert, my son."

Robert started running errands for Fred, who wanted him to keep busy that summer. He rode his big red ten-speed all over Hubbards in the killer heat. It was Nova Scotia's hottest July ever — record highs, they said on the news. We saw more and more of Robert. He'd turn up panting at the Shack between errands, wiping his huge forehead. "Dad, I did that one now, Dad. What do I do now?"

Once, on our lunch break, me and Jason took Robert for burgers. I sat in the back of the pickup as we jostled along; I thought I might bounce right out of the truck. Roads around here don't get paved over too often. Potholes, cracks stay open for years.

Through the rear window I could see Jason chatting with Robert. All I could hear was the roar of the engine, which Jason had been sweating over all summer, making it faster, louder, hungrier for fuel. I watched them, Jason's easy grin, Robert's wide-eyed face, his lips working slowly at each word. Jason can make anyone feel like his best buddy, just like that, with a grin and a couple words and an offer of beer or smokes. He's natural that way.

It used to piss me off a bit, though. I mean, it was kind of like a lie or something. Because whoever it was he was talking to, Robert or Fred or Craig or whoever, that person wasn't his best buddy at all. I was.

When we got to Bob's diner we had burgers with fries to go, in paper bags with big grease stains on the bottom. We sat outside, Jason with his shirt off and his hair falling like black water around his shoulders.

"I like a hamburger," said Robert. "I like fries." He took the biggest bite of his burger I'd ever seen. It was almost gone.

Jason chuckled. "You sure do, Robert. I like 'em too. Watch." And he took a huge bite of his own. He held up his burger and made a big show comparing his bitemarks to Robert's. "Okay, buddy," he said, "you win. I guess you like burgers more than me."

Robert screamed with delight and crushed a plastic ketchup packet in the palm of his hand, splattering ketchup over his legs. Jason grabbed a handful of his own ketchup packets and they horsed around trying to spray each other, until all the ketchup was gone, and they ate their fries plain.

I watched all this, taking small bites.

It wasn't long before Jason asked Fred if Robert could come out with us. Fred trusted us; we worked hard for him. "Sure, boys," he said, "that's fine. So long as you keep him out of trouble. I don't want any trouble coming to my boy."

Jason gave a comforting laugh. "You got it, Fred. We'll take good care of Robert."

"Yeah," I said. Fred looked right at me. Something scared me about his eyes, like he saw some secret. Like maybe I hadn't been working hard enough, or I'd stolen tackle.

"Good," he said. "I appreciate that, boys."

Jason and the Halifax guy tumbled over a log, Jason on top. He pushed the guy's head into the sand and flailed away. A crowd was around them now, hollering. I looked away. It's too much to watch, when he has a guy down like that and won't stop hitting.

A hand touched my arm. It was Robert. "Stop them," he whispered.

Luckily for the Halifax guy, the cops arrived at that moment to bust up the party, the cars' blue and red lights splashing out over the water like trippy lighthouses. As always, they just parked in the gravel lot and stayed there, lights on, waiting for everyone to clear out. That summer even the cops were hot and bored.

Jason smacked the guy's face one more time. "You're one lucky asshole," he said. Then, standing and brushing sand off his pants: "Don't give me shit about my friend. What he does ain't my fault. Or your business."

Craig stopped Jason on the way to the parking lot. He had that awestruck look people get after Jason fights. Like he was half terrified, half in love. "Party at my place," he said.

"Great," said Jason. "We'll pick up some more booze first."

Craig looked at his watch, puzzled. "Where?"

Jason winked. "I got my resources."

Robert's eyes were big and moist as we climbed into Jason's truck. "Can I go home now?" he pleaded.

"Party's just getting started, Robert," muttered Jason, and the driver's-side door slammed shut on their conversation. I hopped back into the box. We swerved through the darkness, the hot air whistling past.

Jason had turned up at the elementary school in Grade 5, a pale, skinny thing with short hair. I noticed him in class right away, his silence. He answered roll call with a grunt, and that was it. I was curious about him, his slouched shape in the back row, the look in his eyes like he was wrestling with a tough math problem written on a wall far away. He caught me watching his eyes, though, and I spun round in my seat and didn't look back again.

Then, as I crossed the soccer field on the way home, he caught up to me, grabbed the straps of my backpack, and threw me to the grass. He pinned my shoulders with his knees. He hit me in the face, again and again, hard and unflagging. I could taste blood spreading on the inside of my cheek. Then he just stopped, looked me over with those eyes. "Why you doing this?" I said. It was all I could do to talk; I wanted to faint. Jason didn't answer. He just got off me and walked away, walked clean off the school grounds and disappeared into the woods.

Through the window, I could see Robert looking around in panic. We had pulled into Seaview Resort, half an hour north of town. It had closed down two years earlier. Some of the cabins had been sold, but mostly the place was deserted. Charred logs littered the grass. A playground rusted where it stood; it looked like cigarette ash, ready to crumble if you sat on the swings or stepped onto the merry-go-round. Skeletons of old trucks lurked further off in the high grass.

It was common knowledge that Al McCarthy went away every summer, took his boat up the coast of Newfoundland to some place he had. Nobody knew exactly why, but everyone figured he was up to no good and left it alone. His cabin was at the edge of Seaview, an old half-derelict thing. Doubtless he kept a good stash of liquor, probably too much to load onto his forty-foot boat. Tonight, Jason figured, we were going to claim some of that stash as our own.

We stumbled down the trail with Jason's flashlight and stopped in a clearing. The cabin was dark; one window reflected the moonlight. It was like an open eye.

"What are we doing, guys? What are we doing?" Robert was grabbing my arm again.

Jason shone his flashlight right into Robert's eyes. That shut him up.

"Okay," said Jason. "Let's get some booze."

Robert cut himself going through the window. Jason had put a crowbar through it and knocked away most of the shards, but somehow Robert got one in his hand. He straddled the empty pane and whimpered.

"Get in there," I hissed from behind him. "You'll cut your balls open." I gave him a shove, but he was heavy. He gripped the window pane with his unhurt hand. The other one was bleeding, thick dark streams running down his palm.

Jason was already inside. His flashlight prowled over plank walls, a TV, a stack of cardboard boxes. He stumbled on something and swore loudly.

"Marty, I'm cut." Robert's voice was almost a whisper.

Jason was back at the window, his flashlight in Robert's face again. "What the fuck's going on?"

"I'm cut, Jason." Robert held out his bleeding hand like a beggar.

Jason took Robert's arm. "Climb inside," he said. "Climb inside and I'll fix you up."

"It hurts."

"*Now*, Robert."

Slowly, Robert lifted his big leg over the sill, and he was in. I got ready to follow, running my hand along the ledge to find a smooth spot. My hand tightened on the pane and I hauled myself up. A light came on. I was halfway in. Four feet away was Robert, clinging to Jason. Drops of blood hitting the floor. Across the room, Al McCarthy stood in a doorway, his rifle pointed at us.

Al was in his boxers, the hair dark as eels on his belly, and I laughed. God knows why, I laughed out loud.

*

They didn't bother to charge us. Around here you don't need to send people to court. Everyone talks, and that's punishment enough. Besides, it turned out Al McCarthy was about to leave town for good. That's why he was still there that night: packing up. He didn't want to deal with the cops any more than he had to. "No harm, no foul," he told them.

But Fred didn't want to see us again. I could barely hear his voice over the phone. "Marty, don't bother showing up Monday. And don't come near Robert, ever."

The summer sprawled and stretched, a worm trying to get across the road. I drank more and more when I went to the beach, until I lost track of what was happening and I woke up somewhere on the shore, huge chunks torn out of my memory.

Sometimes, as I wandered home in the morning, my mouth screaming for cold water, I'd catch sight of Robert on his red bike, racing somewhere. I kept my head down; I don't think he noticed me once.

Jason and I were together more than ever, since no one else was talking to us much. Sometimes we took his truck all the way out to Kennedy Beach to get away from the crowds. We'd smoke up in the back, leaning against spare tires and empty oil cans, watching phosphorescence break with the waves.

That time Jason beat me up after school, I had a black eye for three days. In class I was terrified to glance back, and every moment I thought I could feel his eyes eating into my back.

Later, after the eye went from black to yellow and back to normal, I was wandering alone like I used to, out behind the mall. Jason was there, in the shadow of a delivery bay, smoking. I'd never seen a Grade 5 kid smoking before. He grinned. "How's it going?" he said, like nothing had ever happened.

"Good," I said, backing away.

"Smoke?" He held out a cigarette butt-first, his teeth white in the dusk.

I paused, my eye throbbing. Crickets were beginning, trees turning charred black against the sky. I stepped forward and took the cigarette. Because maybe the black eye was my fault. Maybe I deserved it. Maybe things were okay now, just like Jason's smile promised. We huddled in the shadows and smoked, letting the night get thicker around us.

THE WHALES

Lee D. Thompson

at 3:00 A.M. their songs wake us

Such dreamless sleep is preparation for death; so wake now, my husband, wake now, wake now . . . there is so much to see, here with the living . . .

Clarissa's breath is watery whisper.

. . . wake now, wake now . . . for I have been hearing their songs on the wind from the bay, hearing their songs winding the streets on the wind from the bay . . . hearing them, hearing them, hearing them . . .

Clarissa's voice is singsong syllables.

And is slow to rouse me.

Must I open my eyes? I wish to sleep. What will I see if I open my eyes? This is my home, yes, and this is my bed. And my sleep was not dreamless: I was dreaming of ocean, and I tell my wife I was dreaming of ocean, of dark water, of liquid songs, and she nods, though I do not see her nod . . .

Then you were hearing them too, she says.

I open my eyes and see ceiling: it is striped with silveryblue slatlight. I lay still. I listen.

Yes, I say, I hear songs; I hear the whales taking leave of the heaving ocean; I hear . . . Clarissa?

Yes? What is it?

I think you had better go and wake our Clara. She has been so eager this past week, once the city decreed all streets cleared of nighttime traffic, and since we told her.

Yes, I will wake her. She is old enough to know now.

The bed moves.

Clarissa calls for Clara.

Clarissa calls for Clara again.

And where is my nightdress? I call to Clarissa.

And Clarissa returns and hands me my nightdress.

together, we watch from our lawn

Oh, laments Clara, I wish we had been first. Did you not promise that we would be the first to waken? Yet there are our neighbours on their own front lawn!

Clarissa stands over Clara, hugs her from behind. Well, she says, we will have to blame your father for that, your father who sleeps like death itself.

Did you elbow him?

Oh, I did. But it takes many sharp elbows to rouse your father, who sleeps as if entombed in a deep, dark grave.

Well, I would have elbowed him sharper.

Yes, I am sure you would have.

Clara sighs. She is impatient. But where *are* they? she demands. Their singing is on the wind and it seems so close. It is in my ears. Mother, what if they do not come this way this year? Should we not be farther down? Mayla says the Mall is the best place to be, so should we not be there? Should we not be there at the Mall?

I see that my daughter is distraught, so I tell her to hush. I tell her that this suburb is well known to the whales, has always attracted its fair share of whales, and so we should just be patient. Let us wait, I say; let us be patient. And as I speak these words two awaiting whales crest the hill and rest at the corner of Hilltop and Willowgrove, where their singing ceases. Beneath the high silvery streetlight, glistening and rippled, they are beautiful, of spottled colours.

Spottles! cries Clara.

Clarissa clicks the camera.

Mother, hisses Clara, *you will frighten them away!*

Oh no, Clara, I tell our daughter; whales have no eyes with which to see. How do they find their way, you wonder? They are guided by a deep racial memory of past resting grounds, for their distant ancestors were once landbound, and for millions of years they migrated to these hills by the bay, when the sun was at its highest and the winds carried the salty ocean's endless promise.

The wind stirs Clara's dark hair.

And the whales were much different back then. They had many legs and did not have to undulate over the land to move, as they do now, being so accustomed to the watery parts as they are. And they had long torsos, and were not bladdershaped. And they had a hairy hide, hard goring horns, and eyes fore and aft.

The wind brings the scent of ocean and whale.

Their songs return.

They are coming, whispers Clara.

one whale passes, and so Clara prays

To say that they move with a soft slushing is to say the sound of their movement. It is the sound of moving when wearing too many wet shoes. Yet the undulating whale is not entirely ungraceful.

Next door our neighbours are pointing to the next street over, called Edgehill, where three whales are spotted behind splotches of blackleafed trees. Intently I observe how they move. Clara's gaze is on the approaching pair.

Do they sing only when they go, Father? she asks as if from a great distance.

For the most part, I tell her.

Father?

Yes?

These whales stink.

They smell, I confess, of the deep ocean. One day you will like it, I think. And I think we had better move back a ways, for this first whale as nearly as large as our now empty home . . . Do you feel how its wailsong has trembling fingers in your tiny chest?

A solemn nod from Clara.

A dreamy smile from Clarissa, whose nipples are erect.

And now the first whale is before our warm home, I orate . . . *and now the first whale's song thrombs strongly . . . and now the first whale slushes swiftly past . . . and turns the corner at Bayview and Willowgrove . . . and ascends Bayview's long high hill and is gone, bye bye . . .*

Clara, who is disappointed, faces the second whale.

Father, why is it hesitant?

Hmm, it is a younger whale, I tell my daughter with hidden sorrow; yes, a younger whale. Spottled, certainly, but three quarters white; older whales are always three quarters black.

And it sings a hesitant song, says Clarissa.

Clara coos a sound of sympathy. She wonders if it has lost its way, and I tell her that I think it will find its way.

It is my favourite, declares Clara. It is the best whale in the whole world, she adds with confidence. Oh I wish, I wish . . . I then hear her quickwhispered wisps of words, and I give my wife a curious eyeing.

She is praying, confides Clarissa; our daughter is praying for her favourite whale to find its way.

Yes, I say, to find its way to our lawn, I think.

But we are smiling, for we know it will be effective. The nightair is thrumming with song, with haunting intertwining melody, with harmony that is all prayer, and the younger whale ripples to our driveway, flattens our prickly hedges, and settles in for the night.

Its song, says our daughter, who is delighted, makes my feet tickle.

the secret we have kept

Inside our warm home, our nightdark home, their songs surround us. The glass buffet vibrates, and the wineglasses hum. There is something rattling in the kitchen, warns Clarissa, who takes my hand and leads me there. Don't be alarmed, I tell her; you will only frighten our child. But she is so very tired now, answers Clarissa, and must get some sleep, and I fear the rattling will rattle her nerves. She is very excited, I say, and I do not think she will sleep at all this night. No, says Clarissa, the songs induce sleep in children.

And the children sleep in, I say, recalling a phrase.

We embrace.

The mysterious rattling stops and we hear our daughter's determined snore.

We continue in whispers, harsh whispers, for the songwhales' wailsong surrounds us. So, whispering, we say . . .

Surely you heard what she said?

Oh yes, I heard.

And how are we to tell her?

That she will not be able to play with the whale tomorrow?

Yes. That.

Every family goes through this difficult time, my love.

We are now going through this difficult time, my love.

She will know when morning comes.

Oh, we should wake her and tell her!

No, let her sleep; she will not sleep well if she knows.

Yes, you are right. It is just so sad.

Yes . . . I remember, I remember . . .

I cried for days and days, weeks . . . weeks . . . weeks . . .

Yes, Clarissa, we all remember, we all remember . . .

morning comes, so I go for a walk

My family are asleep now, and through the windows the sun is casting a hard and slanted beam. Inside my home all is sharded, with all glass shattered, so I must step carefully.

136

I did not dream of nothing before I woke.

I did dream.

Of ocean. Of terrible shadows falling heavy through the ocean, shadows of great weight. I lay at the bottom of the ocean and the shadows fell with great weight. I waited at the bottom of the ocean as the shadows fell with great weight and covered me, and I could no longer breathe the ocean air. The shadows lay heavy upon me, and I called out to my wife, *Clarissa, Clarissa,* and she pulled the soft covers from my head, and I saw my home, my bed.

Clarissa will tell Clara.

They say this time of the day only the children hear the songs, the children who are asleep.

I hear nothing; I am not a child.

Outside my home I hear my neighbour, whose name is Axel. Axel is eyeing our whale.

Some whale there, Carl, he says to me.

Some whale here, Axel, I say to him.

Axel sits atop his front step and pulls sparking slivers from his feet.

Our lawnwhale, I see, is half deflated, but breathes still, as frothy blowholes attest. If there is a song, I cannot hear it. But I listen, I try. I move on. Our street is littered with whaleskin, which sticks fast to the asphalt and flaps in the morning wind. When the sun rises and blasts down its rays there will be a difficult odour, I mutter, then move on. I stand at Hilltop and Willowgrove and I have a view. From here I see the Mall parking lot, and it is glutted with whales. I move on down Hilltop and the bay below me is glitterful and blinding. With my hand to my head to cover my eyes I pass the parking lot of deflating whales. That is sacred ground there, I say. I stop. Ahead an exhausted Greatblack is lying in the street — but hooks are in it, and lines tauten, and the whale is dragged away. I move on. The land is level now, the soil is growing sandy, and I hear crashing waves. I move on. I see that the pier has been assaulted, and seems aslant. I move onto the pier. I walk and stop at the edge of the pier, where I stand and I gaze . . .

The ocean is black and impenetrable, and nothing swims there, I say. But I will gaze a long time. And when there comes a breeze my lungs will ache for air, and these dark waters will ripple; and when a white bird skims the water I will pray for the sleeping children, whose hearts are innocent of all this, and who will soon wake to hear the shrill engines of slicing chainsaws . . .

Yes, I say to no one at all, Clarissa will tell Clara.

LEARNING TO SWIM

Larry Lynch

MELVIN REMEMBERS THE FIRST TIME SHE CAME TO HIS apartment; she didn't notice his disorganized desk — there was no time; it was straight into the bedroom, wet bathing suits and all. Since that first time, Melvin thinks she has become more interested in the chaos which is not only his desk but his whole apartment. Melvin imagines she believes it holds in its disarray the answers to who he is and what he *really* wants.

Is this what you do? she asks, standing at his desk. On it is a smorgasbord of worthless office materials, a coffee mug full of pencils and pens, and scraps of paper with phone numbers on them. The shape and crumpledness of the scraps are clues to whom the numbers belong. The bulletin board on the wall above the desk is home to hanging article ideas, notes from interviews, and things that Melvin periodically jots down.

Yes, he tells her. This is it. She scans Melvin's apartment and sees all that it has brought him. Patio furniture. Nintendo. Stacks of paperbacks climbing in the corners and overflowing from cardboard boxes. She picks up a few of the books, remarking that they are all written by the same person, and gives Melvin a peculiar look.

This isn't all just newspaper stuff, she says. She pulls some pages from the bulletin board. Tacks scatter — Melvin's callused feet will find them in the dark some night. She holds some notes about a female firefighter, then she drops them on the desk and pulls down something else. Paragraphs, scenes, and characteristics in point form about a writer Melvin envisions — the writer in the story that Melvin hopes will deliver him from obscurity into the pseudo-obscurity of literary journal fame. She places it on the desk. Go get your shower, she says, you smell like chlorine. She begins to tidy his desk, sort the scraps, stack the mail, and disrupt the chaos. Go on, she urges. She has to be back at the pool in an hour. Aquaerobics. Melvin knows that she's afraid if she is late the priest will find out somehow that she is not Catholic and fire her for lying on her application. Melvin soaps his flabby body. She snoops and reads.

She finds:

For June 14th issue. Run photo. J. Fark 555–1444. Joan Fark hopes to be Middleton's first female firefighter. She is the 35-year-old unwed daughter of John and Missy Fark of Middle Ave. She has been training hard for the physical and is confident she can pass. In a phone interview, Captain McMahan stated he looks forward to seeing her on the crew. The Middleton Fire Department only responded to twelve calls last year.

And this:

When you hear his voice on the radio as you search

in the glove compartment for enough change for a coffee, suddenly he is real. Never have you seen a picture of him on the covers of any of his books. You have been to the bookstore to buy new copies of his work, to see if any of them contain his picture. You have wondered if he may be a she. When you hear his voice it is like finding your birth mother, like finding money in a dirty pair of pants, like the first time your hand felt its way into a bra or had a hand feel its way into yours (if indeed that was a good thing at the time). <———— THIS IS WAY OVER THE TOP, BUT I LIKE THE NOTION OF IT

You hear him avoid answering stupid questions from the radio interviewer who clearly hasn't read his latest book about which he/she now questions him. He changes the subject, and speaks about his boat (he has a boat, you knew it!) and pulls the inept announcer away from embarrassment. But he/she persists. <——GENDER AMBIGUITY, I'LL LEAVE IT FOR NOW. *After a long silence he clears his throat and tells him/her that people who have read his books, read any books, don't fight or fear or question or see as quintessential or heavy-handed every mention of water and the sea; they accept it, embrace it, draw it into their lungs, drink it, breathe it, fuck in it, give birth in it, die in it, make it their own. It is canvas and it is paint. And he says that it is time he should go. You can hear him pushing away from the microphone, and leaving the control booth.*

YOU (and you know who you are . . . hehe)
SEE THE WRITER IN A COFFEE SHOP —
HEAR THE WRITER AND RECOGNIZE HIS
VOICE FROM THE RADIO, BUT DO NOT
SEE HIS FACE, AND FOLLOW HIM IN
YOUR CAR WHEN HE LEAVES.
— *describe car? hair? coffee?*

Melvin's son's feet couldn't touch bottom, so he clung to the side, or to the ladder, or to Melvin's neck. When Melvin pried him away, the little boy swam furiously toward his father with his head tipped back and the white Styrofoam flotation bubble on his back bobbing at the surface. All around them, children flung themselves into the water. Melvin wanted to swim, if he had been able, under the buoys that marked the boundary of the shallow end, to take his son where the water was deep and where there were fewer swimmers. With goggles strapped to his chubby face he could see things floating: hair, snot, Band-Aids. If the water had been clearer he could have seen all the way to the deep end, watched swimmers come crashing through the surface from the diving board, then arch upward, expelling trails of bubbles as they neared the air. But he only lay on his back, on the bottom, and watched his son kick wildly and smile at him with cheeks filled with air.

On a day when there were not too many kids in the pool, a threat of rain perhaps, she spoke to him. She told him that he had to get down into the water with his shoulders submerged when he was instructing his son; something about being less intimidating. Melvin had watched her before; watched her instruct, watched the instructions more than the instructor, watched people learning to swim rather than watching the swimmers, watched their strokes, their progress, the process. His son tried to push off the wall and glide on his front with his face in the water, but couldn't seem to get it right. Show him, she said. Melvin waited for a few kids to move before he pushed his large, sinking body off the wall. It was not graceful. He didn't go far. You don't swim, she said. No. You should take lessons.

You have assumed most successful authors have houses here and there, in one city or another, on lakes and rivers, looking out at the sea, with boats moored, bobbing, tethered, waiting for guidance. When he drives to an average neighbourhood, with average lawns and hedges, you are surprised. Surprised that you have made him something he is not, surprised that you are following the man whose name lives on all the covers in that pile of books in your apartment. Should he stop and walk back to your car, and ask what the hell you are doing following him, you will swallow your tongue, and be the second imbecile that he has had the misfortune of encountering in less than an hour. He parks on the street, locks his car, walks down the sidewalk with a large case under his arm, then plunges into a hedge and scoots across a lawn into a house. A woman closes the door behind him.

    —writer [name? appearance?]
    —novel, masterpiece. "Same Beach. New Waves" ?? ack!

—reclusive, hates to do interviews, promote book
—young writer pursues author, finds him
—alternating POV recluse/young writer
—magic realism?, the bottles/jars

The woman's house has numerous illuminated windows and it reminds you of the bank of televisions at the electronics store, each on a different channel. You see them going from room to room. His back is always to you, or there is some obstruction so you can not see his face. The woman looks young; younger than the back of his head. Every time you come back, and you come back to crouch in the hedge every night when you see his car parked across the street, you watch them struggle, see the case sitting there on the kitchen table.

When the water in the shower hits Melvin's head, the bathroom fills with the smell of the swimming pool. He has often thought about getting more organized. Sometimes he begins to straighten things, but an idea or a story usually sidetracks him. *She* is organized, and the consummate instructor. And after his shower he knows he will be the recipient of more instruction. She's like that: there are two ways of doing things: her way, and the wrong way.

She says she can't orgasm unless everything is just so. She has to be on top. All the blankets must be off the bed — if so much as the sheet is resting on her feet she gets distracted. Once she reaches a certain point, there should be no more talking; she gets an extreme look of concentration on her face as if she is trying to hear and smell and taste and feel and imagine some far-away sensation — one that she has yet to understand or describe but knows exists — and that this way, *her* way, is the only the way to experience it. But she hasn't yet, and Melvin feels that it must be something he is doing wrong, so he tries to be invisible; invisible the way the wind is until it blows newspapers across the street, picks up a trailer park and turns it upside down, or suspends the hem of a dress. (This is something he thought of once, and it is on a scrap somewhere in his apartment.) If there is a rhythm, he tries to sustain it. He watches her face, her closed eyes, trying to draw some instruction from them. He has even tried holding his breath as if he is trying to float.

> *Soon after he arrives you see them pass from window to window. He follows her from the foyer, down the hall to her bedroom. While she gets undressed and puts on a robe, he follows her about, reading to her. A manuscript! You wish you could hear them — him. But you watch. The woman brushes her hair. He holds the vital pages in his hands, waving them emphatically when he reaches an important part. You are dying in the bushes and the woman is brushing her hair. Brushing her hair! Finally she stands and she takes the pages. She reads for a minute, then shrugs, asking him a question. He throws his arms in the air, takes back the pages and turns to leave the room but she whirls him around by his arm and detains him, throws her*

arms around his neck, and kisses him. <——
*CLICHÉ? FRANKLY, SCARLET, I DON'T
GIVE A DAMN.*

*You can see her robe fall to the floor, see the
outline of her breasts against the lamp in her room.
Her belly has a gentle plumpness. She always
undoes his tie, sits him on the bed and removes his
shoes. She takes the pages and sets them aside, then
climbs on top of him, pushing him onto his back.*

On Tuesday evenings there are adult swimming classes.
Kids from the previous lessons hang about outside the
fence and watch the adults wade cautiously into the shallow end. With the exception of Melvin, it looks like a
seniors' class. They seem to come in pairs and threes, pre-
wrinkled men and women who talk and don't listen, who
can already swim in some sort of easy but inefficient
fashion, and seem to be there for recreation, not instruction. That first night they lined up on the deck. The
instructors said they must evaluate each pupil so that the
class could be separated into groups. The first woman
swam across the pool. Her hair didn't even get wet, and
she was directed to the side of the pool with the diving
board. Melvin was the last to go. He got about halfway
across the pool in the shallow end before reaching for the
bottom — first with his hands, then his feet, swallowing
some water as he finally found his footing and stood up.
Two instructors went with the others. She stepped into
the shallow end with Melvin.

Can you float on your front? she said. Like a dead
man? Spread your legs and arms like a star and take deep
breath and relax. He did, and expected if he followed

instructions that he would float right to the top and feel the sun on his back, feel the surface of the water slapping in his ears. The first time, he went down almost to the bottom. His body jackknifed and he lurched to his feet. Relax, she said. Take a deep breath, look at the bottom, spread out, and you will float. Again he sunk, but held his position and found that he rose and floated about a foot under the surface. Did you take a deep breath? Yes. You're a sinker. Some people just aren't floaters.

Try it on your back. He did. Water filled his nose and he beat his arms and legs as if he was falling from a plane. She was giving instructions as he submerged. When he came up, coughing, she was folding her arms across her chest warming herself, then she stretched out and demonstrated how it was done. She floated like suds on water. The tops of her thighs, the round of her face, her breasts, nipples, and the plump part of her belly where her bathing suit stretched flat over the hollow of her belly button were all above water. Look at the clouds, she said, not at your feet. She said this, looking straight at Melvin, not at the sky, and still she floated like a cork.

Again he tried. This time she stood behind him and cradled the back of his head in her hands. A deep breath, she said. He took a deep breath. He felt his chest rising to the surface, but his heels still touched the bottom. Stretch out and look up. He did. Now move your legs a bit. When he did, he found himself on top of the water, concentrating like hell on the sky. There you go. She smiled and let go of his head. He sunk and swallowed more water, a strand of hair.

From his stillness you derive uncertainty. Her pulses and writhing transferred to his rigid frame account for his only movements. Her hair falls into his face when she leans over him to instruct him. She leads his hands to where she wants them. You can see him grope when he should caress, pinch when he should tickle. And when it all should be arriving at some sort of crescendo, she gets out of bed and lights a cigarette. You watch her console him with a light touch on his cheek. You watch him sit on the edge of the bed, his head hung low. She kneels in front of him, smoke curling to the ceiling from her free hand while she attempts to validate him with her other. She does this until the ember burns too close to her fingers and she stops and butts it out in the ashtray on the nightstand.

—JUST SAY IT! BLOWJOB! BLOWJOB BLOWJOB BLOWJOB

—STEREOTYPICAL MALE FANTASY?

—WHAT WOULD MARGARET A. SAY ABOUT ALL THIS?

Melvin dried himself with his last clean towel. Tonight he must go to the Laundromat because tomorrow is his Saturday. Every second Saturday, Melvin and his son walk up the hill to the pool that bingo money built. Melvin carries their lunch, the folding chairs, and the bag with his towel and sunscreen. His son carries his towel and must be reminded constantly not to drag it on the ground. The little boy's head swivels around and he points every time he sees a police car; Melvin assumes, but hopes differently, that the boy has far greater affection, as does his mother, for brawny police officers than flaccid newspaper reporters. The swim starts at one and goes until five. All morning, Melvin's son asks him what time it is, and how long before they go swimming. He wants to go into the parking lot of Melvin's apartment building and throw the Frisbee around, but it is too close to the street and there are too many cars in the parking lot whose scratches Melvin could not pay to get unscratched. Every second Sunday the little boy goes back to his mother.

On Saturday afternoons, fifteen minutes before the swim is over, the priest crosses the lawn of the rectory, clad in his white swim trunks with his towel over his shoulder. He waits on the sidewalk until the traffic stops. He crosses the road, nodding at the drivers, usually calling them by name and making some lame joke about holy water. The hair on his chest is far darker than on his head. It furrows down in a narrow line from his breastbone to his navel, and across his chest from one nipple to the other, forming a cross over his fat gut. He walks past the girl who collects the money and then on deck as kids and parents gather their stuff. He asks the lifeguard if anyone has drowned today. When the lifeguard says no, the priest pats him/her on the back, says, Good boy/girl. He knows Melvin's son. He walks over to them and says, So, your dad is teaching you to swim. Yeah, he says, but we can't go under the rope 'cause my dad can't swim in the deep end. Melvin wishes there was one of those small sliding doors between his voice and the priest's so he wouldn't have to look at the priest's neat face. *I confess to God I can't swim. This is my first confession since my first confession. Can you talk a little louder?* they always say. *Can't swim? Really?* Sign up for some lessons, he tells Melvin, patting him on the back. Melvin grins at him, wondering why he never sees any nuns swimming.

Melvin's son tells him that his mother takes him to church; that is how he knows God. He's not God, Melvin tells him. He just works for him. In any event, Melvin doesn't know the man. He's not the priest that married him, or made his son bawl by dunking his head into a basin of water when he was an infant. Maybe he is — maybe he just doesn't recognize him with his clothes off. Once the pool is empty, but while everyone is still there to see him, the priest dives into the deep end. He glides under water to the shallow end, where he does a flip turn and glides almost all the way back before he comes up for a breath. God is a good swimmer, Melvin's son says. God is going to take a heart attack, Melvin tells him.

—WOMAN LOOKS BORED IN ONE OF THE OTHER ROOMS. SMOKING? TV?

He goes to her with new pages. He reads to her as she smokes and turns the room, and him, from blue to not-so-blue to blue-grey to blue-green. Orange tracers. You wonder if she is even listening. You would listen. Bluish-yellow. Deep purplish-blue, almost black-blue.

He looks frustrated. You hate her. He leaves the room, walks past the room where he writes, down the hall, past the bathroom, into the kitchen. He puts the mysterious case under his arm and goes back to his typewriter.

—the MYSTERIOUS case . . . needs description?

While Melvin is drying himself she walks in and holds out what she has been reading. What's this all about? she says.

What is it?

She begins to read: *You can see her robe fall to the floor, see the outline of her breasts against the lamp . . .* Who is You? You or me? Or is this smut supposed to be us? She is not smiling. Melvin is naked.

It could be both, he says, and neither.

And is there something else you want to ask me? To say to me?

No.

No?

No.

Blowjob? Blowjob blowjob blowjob?

As true as it is, Melvin knows his explanation is not going to fly as he hears himself speak the words. It's nothing like that, he tells her. It's unfinished. It's something I've been playing around with. Her expression doesn't change, and he knows she is trying to decide if he is lying or crazy.

You're not fooling anyone, she says. She studies the pages. Who is Margaret?

Margaret Atwood. He wraps the towel around his waist.

Sure it is. Is my belly really plump?

Not at all, he says. I make some of it up. It's fiction.

Well, she says, some of it seems okay. She finally smiles, then she hugs him, the wet towel between his belly and hers.

The light by which he types silhouettes him. By this time you can see that his hands combing through his hair have left it standing in places. His shirt is untucked, wrinkled. He rips paper from the machine and crumples it. Glorious scraps. He writes in short bursts, reads what he has written, writes more, then discards it. You can see him pacing around the room, but with the light to his back it is his shadow you would be able to recognize anywhere, not his face.

Two, then three circuits around the room. The woman continues to bathe in blue. He peeks into the hallway, then ducks back into his room and closes the door. Looking over his shoulder — listening for her — you assume, he carefully opens the case, withdrawing jars and holding them up to the light, inspecting their labels. From selected jars he removes the lids, reaches in with his fingers, and plucks out some of the contents and releases them into the air over his head. He puts the jars back in their place, closes the case, and returns it stealthily to the kitchen. After stretching his scalp with his hands and inserting a clean page, he writes.

It took weeks, but with some constant swirling motion with his hands, and a gentle kicking movement from his knees down, he learned to stay on top of the water on his back and move around the shallow end a bit without touching the bottom. Though it was not graceful, he even learned to roll from his front to his back, his eyes and mouth wide when his face turned to the sky, hoping he was above water where he could take a breath.

Next came the side glide. If he could learn to master it, she told him, it wouldn't be long before he would be learning strokes and swimming lengths of the pool. She demonstrated. First she grasped the side of the pool with one hand, and put her feet against the wall ready to push off. Now watch, she said. Push off the wall, keep this arm out straight, and put your ear against your shoulder. Look back and up a bit, and kick, you have to kick. She glided away from the wall, her legs stirring the water, her head resting on the shoulder of her outstretched arm, and her face completely out of the water. Now you try.

Melvin tried repeating all the instructions in his mind as he gripped the side with one hand and planted his feet onto the wall, ready to push off. There is a part of Melvin that keeps all these seemingly simple components from coming together at once to form what even slightly resembles a swimmer, a stroke. Either his ear is not against his shoulder, his body is too tense and not extended enough, his head is turned the wrong way, or he is not kicking hard enough — or not at all. The result is a mouthful of water and an instance of panic as he splashes and gasps to his feet.

Swallow enough water for today? she asked him as she checked her watch.

To you he looks drained. You would like to see him take his pages, dozens of them since he opened the jars, and leave. Turn out all the lights, pull the plug on her TV and leave. But he takes them to her. He begins to read, and she stops doing nothing and listens. The more he reads, the more attentive she becomes; she sits straighter, sets aside the remote, and extinguishes her cigarette. Before he is done, she takes the pages from him and paces about reading the final pages aloud. You can see her lips *moving. You think he looks too tired to sit, as if a stiff breeze could blow him over, scatter him like leaves. <—— I LIKE IT! When she is done, she sets it aside and smiles.*

He picks up the pages and you can tell he is asking if she liked it. Yes, her mouth moves, and she drops her robe again. Really? his shoulders say. She kneels to undo his pants. He finds a specific page and points out a passage to her and re-reads it.

His back is to you and you see the outline of the tail of his shirt, the crumpledness of his pants, which rest below his knees. In one hand he holds the passage, in the other the smoky blueness of her hair. Only you can't see his face.

—His sleeping face?
—His annoyed face?
—Frustrated?
—Ecstatic?

For the first time he pictured him, saw his face. It was familiar but puzzling. When he lay still, with his arms extended and his eyes closed, not watching her at all, he saw him sitting over his typewriter. He got up from time to time and went into the kitchen. He selected jars of characterization, or maybe symbolism. They were like spices. He reached in and pinched the right amounts of irony, satire, or narrative distance between his fingers and released them into the air like ashes or magic dust. Again and again he tossed his fingers into the air. His face hopeful, familiar. There was a rhythm that Melvin could not understand and did not interrupt. But *she* did.

I see you felt it too, she whispered into his chest. You finally got it right, she said. You did it. *We* did it.

His face was not hard or concerned, as it had been when he tried to write it before. It was unconventional and smooth. It was clean and shiny and even a bit smug; it was familiar and Melvin felt that he should know him, and that if he could remember who he was, then he could give him more reality than he had himself.

What are you doing? she said as she shook him by the shoulders. Melvin opened his eyes. Wasn't it great? she said, and stretched out on top of him.

I could see him, he told her.

Who?

The writer. My character.

That's what you were you thinking of? She wrapped a sheet around herself and got out of bed.

What? he said. Did I miss something?

Nothing, she said. I was faking it anyway. She left. End of lessons.

Melvin's son is taking lessons. Every second Saturday, Melvin sits with his feet dangling in the shallow end and watches the line of children at the deep end, his son included. The first in line steps closer to the side. An instructor treads water a few feet from the edge and holds a flotation ring in one of his hands. The children jump into the water, bob to the top, and grasp the ring. With a slight nudge, the instructor propels them toward the side of the pool; the kids swim with their heads back and with quick, puppy-like strokes to the ladder where they climb out and go to the back of the line. The priest still comes for his dip when the kids are finished.

Yesterday, Melvin watched him as he patted his son on his wet head. He dropped his towel by the diving board and picked some lint from the hairy cross on his chest. With pinched fingers he raised his hand into the air and released the lint into the breeze. Him. It was him.

SAINT BRENDAN'S

R. M. Vaughan

STERLING POKED HIS INDEX FINGER GINGERLY INTO HIS palm and separated the dimes, nickels and quarters into bright pools. He began to count.

"I'd never cheat yah," Mrs. Hutches chided him from behind the counter. "Not on purpose."

Sterling looked up, red-faced. Mrs. Hutches folded her left hand under her right armpit and waited.

"Sorry. Uh, no, of course, no — I — nothing meant. I," Sterling stuttered. He sighed and shovelled the tinkling pile into his front pocket. "Habit. City habit."

Mrs. Hutches leaned forward on her cash register and pretended to dust the top with the end of her sleeve. "You're Hartley's son, aren't you? Hartley Burchill, from Black's Mountain. Your mother was—"

"Ida. Yes, Hartley and Ida," Sterling smiled cautiously.

"Nice pair, them two. Always so polite." Mrs. Hutches looked down at Sterling's empty, sweating hands. "Do anything for you, Ida would."

"Yes, she would." Sterling put his hands behind his back, rubbed one palm against the other. The skin between his fingers felt gummy and fat. "She was a giver, Mum was, a giver." Sterling felt a thin line of stinging sweat inch down his flabby ribcage and over his wide, soft middle.

Mrs. Hutches straightened herself, flattened her yellow blouse. "Not many like her." Mrs. Hutches stared at Sterling's face, her eyes stopping at his flat, indented chin.

"You look like Hartley. Neck up. But he was always so thin, Hartley was. Just a rail."

Sterling turned to leave.

"How long you up home for?"

"I'm here until September."

"That long?"

Sterling nodded.

"Took one of the stilt cottages, didja? Right down on the beach?"

Sterling smiled.

"Till September?"

"End of September."

Mrs. Hutches nodded back.

"Then we'll be seeing you again."

Sterling smiled, shifted his white plastic shopping bag from hand to hand. His left thumb caught on the loops. He felt the end of his thumb swell, fat with stopped blood.

"Do they still call you Sterling, or didja take another name?"

"I'm still Sterling."

"Just as well," Mrs. Hutches winked, "the old names."

Sterling said goodbye and bumped his way out the front door.

Halfway down the meadow to his beachside cottage,

Sterling turned to look back at the store—the familiar pale blue front steps, the cobalt blue and white Hutches General sign, the lottery posters in the window, the hand made notice "Eggs, $1.59 doz," the wiry lilac bushes beside the alley, the single, tin cone lamp above the front door that would be surrounded by furious insects from dusk until the first purple of morning, the high, leaded glass windows that sagged in the center, the spare, undecorated and mean effortlessness of it all, the bald, ever-present fear of ostentation, of grandness or even simple pride.

Mrs. Hutches stood in front of her spindly wooden counter and watched Sterling, watching him make his way down the meadow. She poured a cupful of salt onto the floor where he'd stood.

The small, muddy cove and linked chain of deep, cold, red sandstone ponds at the centre of Saint Brendan's, New Brunswick, are not remarkable, except for the silt. Greenish-grey, thick as fudge, and putrid as the bowels of a dogfish, the silt lines the cove, smothers the rocks, and clings to the clapboard fishing boats like a wet, sucking moss. The bottom of each sparkling pond is a dead, fathomless jade eye; a place for eels to hatch, for bulrushes to stunt and fail, for children to lose watches, toy boats, deflated beach balls, siblings.

On sunny days, the silt glistens, appears peppered with triangular flecks of new copper. But with the nightly fogs comes a pulsing smell. The perforated skin of the silt vibrates, exhales. Bubbles of trapped gas and filth expand and pop, filling the night air with the scent of greasy anvils, boiled feathers, and, on warm evenings, vinegar.

In the late 1970s, the province tried to scrape the harbour clean. Massive bulldozers and chugging front-load diggers, on lease from Maine, invaded the narrow roads of Saint Brendan's for three wretched, rain-blasted summers. The workers — none of them locals, who knew better — staged two illegal strikes, the second lasting all of July. At the end of the third summer the government changed and the project was abandoned. The truckloads of silt dumped high in the woods behind neighbouring Maynard's Corner killed several families of deer and eleven acres of juvenile spruce trees. Porcupine, rabbit, and raccoon tracks discovered at the edge of the green pancakes of mud ended mysteriously in the centre of the blotch.

Within a year of the failed experiment, the silt replaced itself with a new, thicker skin. Guest Relations Officers at provincial tourism kiosks were told unofficially, in both official languages, to gently alert visitors to the equally parochial charms of St. Lucy's or St. Joseph's or Pecan Cove — to anywhere but Saint Brendan's, where the locals (maddened, it is believed, by generations of raw stench, isolation, and relentless, creeping muck) were the mistrusted subjects of unflattering whispers in the otherwise careful halls of government.

From this literal backwater Sterling Burchill emerged, at seventeen, determined to run and run until his lungs cleared. He borrowed money and became educated, patiently learned the ways of European restaurants and how to iron a shirt. He married, made children, collected friends, became estranged. By the age of forty, Sterling had wholly forgotten himself and his boggy beginnings in a thousand tiny turns. Saint Brendan's, however, was timeless.

At the bottom of his soap-stained leather shaving kit, Sterling found the orange bottle of pink pills. He popped one into his mouth and swallowed it dry. He waited. The prescription usually took a full twenty minutes to unravel its knot of complex proteins and bind his nervous system in a tight, calming hug, but tonight he felt the first soft pinch within seconds. The pill left a scorched taste on the back of his tongue. He sat down in a wide, dusty armchair and breathed deeply through his mouth. He was all right again, all right.

Balancing an old atlas across his lap like a table, Sterling took a blank sheet of powder blue paper and laid it on the cover. He chose a pen from a tin can and began to write. He stopped, crumpled the paper, and replaced it with a fresh sheet. He fidgeted in his seat, tucked his elbows into his sides, and wrote the date on the top right-hand corner of the sheet. He exhaled, scratched his thigh, noticed the chair's musty smell, and then worried for an instant, in rapid succession, about fleas, ticks, sand chiggers, nesting garter snakes, and mice. He remembered the smiling man who'd rented him the plywood cottage, who smelled like gasoline. What was behind that smile? Sterling's stomach made a coiling sound. He suddenly imagined the underside of the raised cottage swamped by the midnight high tide; saw the thin, mouldy stilts sagging like wet bread; saw himself crushed and bloody and drowned beneath a pile of greased beams, bent nails, and kelp.

No, stop, Sterling, he told himself. No, stop it.

He filled his cheeks with air, counted to fifteen, made a pinhole with his lips, and let the air whistle out slowly. He began to write.

Dear Kelly,
I guess I forgot how cold the summers are at St. B's.
I should have packed a windbreaker and another
pair of long pants. Could you mail
Sterling crossed out the half-sentence.
How are the kids? Tell them their Dad thinks about
them all the time. How did Marisa do on her math
exam? Is Hedley still coughing? Don't let him out-
side on smog days. Sorry — I guess you know that
already.

I'm not lonely yet — ha, ha. I'm working my
way through all the P.D. James books your father
left you. I feel better.

Yesterday I borrowed an old skiff and made my
way to the end of the cove. The water was dark,
almost black. You'd hate it. The cove used to be full
of seals, but they're all gone. I thought I saw one,
just a head in the water, but it was only some lost
tackle. I'd like to see something I could tell the kids
about. A porpoise, a skate. It's too much to hope for
a whale.

Tomorrow I'm taking the skiff to the other side.
An old salty dog at the harbour told me to look
around the low cliffs for seals. "And if you see one,"
he said, "shoot it."

I'm getting stronger every day. I know how you
worry, but this is the best thing for me right now,
this quiet time.

Well, more seagoing adventures later – ha ha!
Love, Sterling.

Sterling slid the atlas off his lap and reread the letter. Apart from the bit about the cold weather, it was all lies.

Three weeks later, Kelly Burchill found a soggy envelope in her mailbox. Postmarked from New Brunswick, the envelope contained a shattered blue crab leg, a short length of brine-coated netting, a handful of flat, rubbery seaweed leaves, and a dollhouse bundle of driftwood bound with a twist tie. She did not show the package to her children.

Sterling stood at the top of the dune beside his cottage, watched the green waves hit the beach below, then bent over to untie his shoes. A beam of low, western sunlight poked through a fat cloud and lit up the grey sand beneath his feet. The sand glinted and winked. Sterling plopped down and scooped up a sparkling clump. Scales, he thought. The sand is full of scales, fish scales. The sunlight broke out in force and the sand instantly brightened, flickered like a thousand broken prisms, covering Sterling's chest and stomach with purple, yellow, and blue rays. Sterling dropped the clump and stood up. He dusted his backside and stumbled toward the waves. His hands felt itchy, white static sparks jumped up and down his arms.

At the water's edge, between the tide and the sand, sat a wide line of filthy chartreuse silt. The silt was clotted with mussel shells, crab parts, and whole baby lobsters, seagull feathers, seagull wings, what looked like a dog's leg. Sterling found a stick and poked deep into the muck.

The muck pulled back, breaking the stick. Sterling found a bigger stick and shoved it into a fat, heaving mound. Warm air poured out of the hole, smelling like sugar and eggs, like vomit. Sterling left the stick upright in the silt, pulled the neck of his T-shirt over his nose and walked away. The silt burbled behind him.

I'm going crazy, Sterling said out loud. Just like my dad, and my granddad and just like the last time, just like — Sterling shut his mouth. He exhaled slowly and sped along the beach.

Just like the last time, he whispered, with the water pipes, the viruses in the water pipes, and me walking around the house plugging the taps with cement glue, I had to, and bathing the kids in a tub of club soda for safety, and brushing their little teeth with distilled water and the Saran Wrap, I had to, the Saran Wrap on the toilet seat, and then . . . and then I hit Hedley, I hit Hedley, I hit Hedley right on the mouth, I slapped little Hedley for eating an ice cube—

Sterling felt a sharp, painful jolt run up his spine. He lifted his right foot and pulled a long, jagged scale out of his heel. The scale glowed, warm and milky as a pearl. He held his foot up to the last hint of the sun. No blood, not a dribble. A clean cut. Sterling put his head down and walked on, dodging the rumbling mounds of filth and silt, some the size of balloons.

Darkness fell and dulled the colours in front of Sterling's face. The twinkling sand looked like a flat stack of wet, burnt paper. The calico rocks hid their shiny quartz veins, became black bumps. The bright, variegated grass at the edge of the meadow turned blue and curled inward, away from the tide. Everything meant to sleep slept. Sterling bumbled ahead, filling his pockets with blue, transparent scales that cut holes in the fabric of his shorts, nicked his fingers.

He heard Mrs. Hutches' voice and looked up. At the far end of the beach, two or three hundred murky yards from where he stopped, a dozen people stood in a perfect circle. Local people, dressed in plain clothes, knit caps, and sweaters. Mrs. Hutches stood closest to the water. She raised her arms and said something low and rough. Sterling heard, or thought he heard, Mrs. Hutches say "mercy," or "menace," then "gift" — or was it "great," maybe "guard"? Something with a gee sound.

Sterling put one foot forward, right into a low slick of muck. He stepped back, wiping his foot on the sand. A man at the top of the circle came toward Mrs. Hutches with a canvas bag in his hand. Sterling strained to see. Did the bag wiggle?

Sterling heard a low, growling sound. The bag swung from side to side. Inside the bag, an animal shrieked. The man handed the bag to Mrs. Hutches, pulled his hat down over his eyes, and returned to his place in the circle. Mrs. Hutches lifted the bag over her head. The bag churned. Sterling heard the canvas tear.

Mrs. Hutches faced the water and tossed the howling bag high and far into the tide. The bag landed with a dead thump, not a splash, then rolled over once and sank. There were no bubbles.

The men and women in the circle held hands for a moment, roughly and without affection, then broke away in different directions. The tall grass swallowed their footsteps.

*

Kelly Burchill sat at her desk and looked around, listened. The office was empty for lunch. She unwrapped a cheese-and-veggie sandwich and picked indifferently at the lettuce. She opened a new file on her computer, titled it STER, held her breath for a moment, then turned back to her sandwich. A spoonful of black olive slices slid out from between the cheddar and the green peppers, leaving a vinegary pool on her blotter. She popped one into her mouth. It was soft and watery, like a pickled fish.

"Dear Sterling," Kelly began, then backspaced over the letters. Just "Sterling" would do.

> *Sterling,*
> *Do I really need to tell you that I'm worried? Are you that out of it? You've been at St. Brendan's for half the summer now and you're not getting any better as far as I can tell. You shouldn't be there in the first place.*
>
> *I remember you told me once that the reason you got out of St. Brendan's was because nothing ever changed. And now you're sitting there waiting for something to change. People change themselves, Ster - places don't change people. Look at all our friends who spend a fortune on trips to Nepal and the Mexican pyramids and Paris and they come back and they're <u>exactly the same.</u> We used to laugh at them. You said they were fools.*
>
> *I'm not trying to guilt you, but the kids miss you a lot and they're starting to ask questions. Do you want to end up like your father, afraid to leave the house and hiding in the basement all day*

carving the story of Jonah and the whale into the floor? Do you want to go crazy? Is that a <u>goal</u> for you? And don't give me any more crap about confronting your demons. There's no such thing as demons — there's people who know how to act right and people who need to learn and you are category # 2.

Ok, so, let's say for argument's sake that you are right, that there is something back there for you to conquer or face down or whatever. I already know what it is and so do you — you had a shitty childhood because your dad was a nutcase and he drowned himself and we're all very sorry about it <u>but now is now</u> and you've got to decide whether or not you want to live in the past or the present. You have two children who need you. Hedley doesn't even really remember that you hit him. The worse thing is that you hit him <u>and then you fucked off</u>, ran away to the seaside and now Hedley doesn't have a daddy and he thinks it's his fault. Marisa misses you too, but she's in tap camp so at least she's occupied.

Basically, Sterling, I'm putting you on a time line here. If you're not home by the time I get back from Mom and Dad's place in Mimico I'm going to see Mr. Harwood about a separation. I won't say divorce because I believe in giving people a chance.

Love,
Kelly

Kelly printed the letter and sealed it in a company envelope. She went to the supply closet and stole some stamps. She licked the stamps, stuck them on the envelope, left the building, and tossed the letter in a mailbox. On her way back she bought a Diet Coke. Her mouth tasted like burnt salt.

While the old moon lasted, Sterling watched. Every night the same villagers gathered on the beach, formed a circle and tossed a wailing bag into the surf. Hidden behind a high dune, Sterling tried to guess the different animals by their sounds. Raccoon, porcupine, raccoon, three or four cats, fox, mutt dog, raccoon again, a baby deer. Mrs. Hutches always led the ceremony, and by the third night Sterling figured out most of what she called out to the waves in her low, uneasy voice. A guardian was summoned, a guardian was paid.

Sterling stopped sleeping at night. Between the early morning light and noon he forced himself to lie down and submit to a couple of hours of restless drifting. He half dreamed of his children — his sweet, chubby children — and of boats — long, slender, and graceful boats with polished metal oars that felt like knives in his hands. He never dreamed of Kelly or any other woman, but he often pulled himself out of near dreams of shadows — huge, bottomless shadows that moved under his feet while he stood on a clear glass floor or walked on water. The shadows heaved and snapped beneath him, curvaceous and swollen and flirty.

The afternoons were spent collecting scales. Sterling started from the low, rocky beach in front of his cottage and traced a thorough west-east circle from the sandy, grass-tufted dunes at the cove's high end to the sticky pools at the cove's bottom. He found hundreds and hundreds of jagged scales in dozens of colours and crammed

his shredding pockets full. On the floor beside the fire-
place he sorted the scales by predominant colour —
bottle green, black, shiny black, or glossy pink. The
piles grew taller and ranker, but Sterling only noticed
their gleam, the way they continued to shine long after
the sun had set. A week passed, then another.

On the last afternoon of his life, Sterling fell asleep
on the floor beside his scale collection, deeply and truly
asleep. He dreamed of warm hugs, of being surrounded
by loving arms. He dreamed of Hedley, of his baby boy's
smiling, upturned face. He dreamed of a rain of hot
tears, a scalding, cleansing rain. He dreamed of Jonah
and the whale, of Jonah's happy life inside the whale's
belly, where the walls were soft as flannel. He dreamed he
was wrapped in steaming, wet towels.

Covered in sweat, Sterling awoke three hours later
on the other side of the room, in the dark, with his arms
twisted under his back and his body stuck with scales.

Sterling drew a hot bath and gently plucked off the
scales. The scales left bright yellow holes in his thighs
and itching, bloody slices on his back. He poured a
whole bottle of rubbing alcohol into the bath water and
lowered himself into the foam. The water turned orange,
rust orange, then dusty grey.

Dressed in a plaid shirt and long shorts, Sterling
wandered toward the meeting place, the circle. The sky
was clear and pocked with stars, and in a few minutes
Sterling reached his hiding place behind the dune. The
villagers were just beginning to form the circle. They did
not speak or nod or shake hands. Sterling cupped his
hands over his ears and waited for the familiar chants.
The beach was silent and cold.

Mrs. Hutches stepped into the centre of the circle and lowered her wide arms.

"Sterling, come down," she called.

Sterling stood up stiffly and gave the circle a shy wave.

"Come down."

The circle broke open at the top, making a hole for Sterling. He walked into the middle and faced Mrs. Hutches.

"Good boy, Sterling, good boy. You was always a good boy, an awful good boy."

Sterling began to cry. A man left the circle and stood beside Sterling. With dry, chipped fingers, the man quickly undressed Sterling. Good boy, Sterling, Mrs. Hutches whispered, sleepy boy. The man's touch was kind and careful. He held Sterling by the back of the neck and smoothed his hair. Sterling looked down at his naked body and felt nothing — not embarrassment, not shock, not arousal, not fear, not calm.

Mrs. Hutches took Sterling's hand and lead him to the water's edge. She held his shoulder as he stepped into the white, bubbling tide. She walked with him until the hem of her skirt was wet and sticking to her knees. She gave him a gentle shove and Sterling dove into the water head first.

Sterling opened his eyes and blew bubbles out of his nose. He looked down into the dark. The sand below was carpeted with scales, blinking like fireflies. Sterling swam farther and deeper. Ahead of him, just out of sight, the sand rumbled. Scales twirled and arched in a cloud of mud and twigs and rocks. Sterling pumped his legs and ploughed through the debris. The water grew still again.

Sterling came up for air. He turned and saw the villagers holding hands, their circle as perfect as a drawing. He paddled ahead and felt a piece of seaweed tickle his calves. He kicked it away. Another long, clammy leaf brushed his stomach. He swivelled and bucked, but the seaweed tightened across his torso. Sterling lifted his knees for balance and took a deep breath. He smelled rust — rust and piss and salt and, yes, that too, yes, blood.

The sea broke open. A panel of scales — live, veined, bristling scales — passed in front of Sterling's face and sank away. His mouth filled with a thin, oily slime. Sterling gagged and thrashed. The body rose again, higher than before. Sterling saw muscles under the scales and the trace of a long, wide rib cage. A fin as big as car door patiently slapped the surface.

Sterling pissed himself. The creature bent its body against the waves, sheltering Sterling from the rough tide. Sterling screamed. The creature encircled him, made its hide into a tall funnel. Sterling splashed and kicked frantically in the still pool, surrounded by a high wall of scales and muscles and steaming skin. He grabbed at a slippery flank and tore off a handful of scales. Angry bubbles broke around his head. He reached for the bare spot of skin and dug in with his nails. The creature wrapped a leathery fin around Sterling's head, jerked it backward, and snapped his windpipe. Sterling sank lazily into the creature's mouth.

Kelly unlocked the front door of the cottage and found it had been swept clean and washed with bleach. Mrs. Hutches, she guessed. Kelly opened some windows and began to pack up her drowned husband's clothing.

Shoving a dirty plaid shirt into a duffle bag, she felt a keen sting in her palm. A trickle of blood ran down her index finger. Cursing and furious, she shook the shirt. A clump of damp string and shells fell out of the pocket. She unwound the clump and laid three perfectly knotted shell necklaces flat on the bed. Sucking her palm, she counted one long necklace, for her, and two smaller strings, one for Hedley and one for—

Kelly sat down on the bed and cried.

An hour later, she finished packing Sterling's books and shoes. She gingerly picked the necklaces up by their ends and threw them into the alders behind the cottage. The children would only cut themselves on the shells.

CONJUGAL APPROACHES

Kelly Cooper

THIS NAUGHTY BOOK YOU'VE GIVEN ME, THIS HOW-TO book, perhaps a joke, perhaps not, is by no means the first such book I've ever read. The first was called *Sexology*. Puritan Publishing Company. 1904. I found it lying in plain view, on the floor of my great-grandparents' abandoned farmhouse, dull green cover marked by the white droppings of sparrows that flew in through gaps in broken window glass. I hid it beneath my coat so no one would see.

My great-grandparents were dead before I was born. There is one photograph. An unsmiling, already old woman in a strange and shapeless knitted cap. A man, skin dark from weather, a white shirt buttoned tightly at his throat. There are stories about eighteen hour days and six cows milked before breakfast. What use would they have had for a book like this?

Of course, they were doing it, I know that, everyone knows that. All of them, even then. Great-grandparents, grandparents, parents. Nothing to wonder about. The mystery is a tired man bent over a book in a cold dark room, his lips moving to sound out the word *libertine*. A woman lying awake, forearms aching from the twice-a-day pull of cows' teats, waiting behind a makeshift curtain for the man to come to bed. The mystery is the reading.

The book is a study in euphemism. I have it still, read it for words like *onanism* and *thraldom* and quaint turns of phrase. It is the duty of the husband to at all times assure his wife is apt for conjugal approaches. There are no pictures. It has theories, some strange and unproven, some not. A passage reads, "Nature has decreed that the act of reproduction shall be expensive to the individual, so she surrounds it, in all cases, with something more or less of danger." Unequivocal. That much, at least, made clear.

Make no mistake. Yours are not the first love letters I've received. When I was in sixth grade, a boy sent me notes. A dirty-faced boy with eyes that glittered blue as sun on water. He wrote, Who do you love? I love you, and signed with x's or with o's. Sometimes with both. I read these in a small cubicle of the girls' bathroom, with two friends who advised me. Write back, they said, his eyelashes are long and curly. Three of us jammed into the tiny space. Bodies touching here and there. Closer to each other than we'd ever yet been to boys. Air sweet with wild strawberry.

I didn't know how to sign. Did not want my reply to give him bold ideas. Did not really want to write to him at all, but urged by my friends, I printed small questions in reply, What is your favourite colour? Who is the prettiest girl in grade six? More for their approval than for his. Then the closing. X? O? I could not keep straight which meant hug and which meant kiss. Even if I had known, the decision was not easy. A kiss could be a disembodied touch of lips to lips, like children give old women who are familiar to the family. Or it could be something else. Foreign. French. A hug could be more like just friends, but it meant a sort of full-length touching. Bodies touching. Didn't know. Did not want to let on to my friends. Wrote back to the boy and signed both. The start of giving too much away.

I thought I had hidden the notes in undiscoverable places, but my mother found them. We need to have a little talk, is what she said. The birds and the bees, my mother called it. Vague intimations of flutters in the stomach and lower. I thought I knew how I'd been made. Life shimmered, transparent as insect wings.

Yours is very nice, don't get me wrong, but I've seen others like it. Its shape and weight are not as unique as you assume. Don't be fooled by blushes or averted eyes. A woman's cheeks grow red for many reasons. One time, a boy exposed himself to me on the school bus. I'd known him all my life. Not the blue-eyed boy. Another. He tried to lay hands on me at every opportunity. Hands I liked, but would not admit to liking. A date was what I wanted. Not that kind of girl, I led him to believe, but it wasn't virtue. Didn't know. Again. After the hands, what then? One day I turned in my seat, turned my back against him until he called my name. I love you, he said and when I turned to face him, he grabbed my hand. Forced it down to where he was unzipped. Felt smooth. Surprised by how smooth. And such an odd colour. Soft purple like the mark left by grapes crushed against a white cloth. There, he said. There. You won't have to see another one of those until you're married. And he never

asked me. Him, I loved. I'd have marked his skin with
slow x's, if I'd known then what I know now.

Not long after, I overheard my parents talking about
the neighbour's baby girl. An accident, they called her.
Puzzled me. I knew the strength required for the boy to
move my hand, just my hand, to that part of him. Yet it
seemed the act could be performed without volition.
Like bees can't help returning to the hive. Happening
perhaps in sleep. A vivid dream.

The author of *Sexology* (a man with a splendid mous-
tache and a high, starched collar, Wm. H. Walling, A.M.,
M.D.) advises readers, "remember that a woman has her
capacity for sexual enjoyment, and most, if not all, have
a tender spot for a child and a perfectly natural desire to
become a mother." True, in my case. There are children I
have wanted. When I was in college, I fell in love with the
lab assistant. Biology lab. Yes, I do. I do recognize the
irony. Admired him bent over a microscope. Legs were
magnificent. He'd played soccer in every province in
Canada. Had played in Europe. He was older. Bearded.
Experienced. A woman is safe from pregnancy, he
claimed, as long as she doesn't climax. So I fought pleasure. Imagined myself a stone. A brittle skin of ice over
water. Didn't help. Didn't work. How do you know it's
mine? he asked. The trophy was on his desk. A man covered in false gold, his leg extended to kick a ball, balanced
on a heavy marble base. I swung it hard. He moved
quickly, shifted so the trophy missed his head, which is
why he is alive, why he lives on today and will continue
to live without thinking of me very often, until the arthri-
tis creeps through his body and settles in the once

cracked collarbone. His wife will rub his shoulders and ask sympathetically, what is the matter? And he will say, nothing, just an old injury from my sporting days. Not a complete lie.

And then there wasn't one after all. No baby. Thirty percent of women miscarry. Natural and unexplained in most cases. Like an abandoned hive. Unused honeycomb of cells for no reason. Nature numbers things in trillions. I was not alone. Not completely.

Wm. H. Walling's eyes are kind and rather sad. Perhaps he expects no one to listen when he recommends marriage as a remedy against debauch. Perhaps he suffers from his own advice, "The rule should be for the one who loves the most to measure his ardour by that of the one who loves the least." Maybe he would like to leave his wife.

Most of my life, sex has been a story poorly told. Vague. Images blurred by metaphor like hot breath steams a mirror. Birds and bees. I've come to back to that, my mother's old-fashioned way of telling it. Watch me unfold, my body like wings. Breasts swell, soft throats of birds. For singing. I am ready for song. Bands of sunlight shine through blinds. Shadows stripe your torso. Feel my fingers, single feathers, drifting light upon your skin. Now close your eyes, your Wm. Walling eyes, kind and rather sad and much, much less resigned. You are the bee, I guess, stinger rising bluntly from your belly. Bees do not survive the stinging. Leave parts behind. Die from need of them. Think about that. Hesitate.

I have a good memory. I remember useful things. Things amusing and otherwise. I can quote Wm. H.

Walling, "If we search the entire animal kingdom we shall everywhere find the female stamped with the seal of physical subordination, save in the cases of certain birds and insects." Subordinate save in certain cases. Fair warning. Let it be clear. You are not the first. Before you enter. Before you do. Remember. The leaving will kill you.

THAT FALL

Michael Crummey

THEY FOLLOWED THE HEARSE IN THROUGH THE COUNTRY
from St. John's, four hours on the Trans-Canada to Notre
Dame Junction, the weather cold but surprisingly fine
for mid-December, the roads clear. At the Junction they
turned north off the main highway, driving on to
Twillingate, where Grace's mother was scheduled to be
buried the following morning.

At the funeral home the driver of the hearse
walked with them across the crushed-stone parking lot
to the door. She was a young woman just out of mor-
tician's college, no more than twenty-three. She wore
black slacks and a short black blazer with the cuffs
turned up at the wrists. Grace asked, "Was Mom any
trouble on the drive?" and the girl smiled. She had
small, perfect teeth. "No my love," she said. "She was
good as gold."

When she disappeared into an office down the hall,
Ed said, "She seems happier than someone in her job has
a right to be."

"She's just a youngster," Grace told him.

Ed leaned toward Grace's son Isaac, who had flown
in from Houston for the funeral. "She'll never have to
worry about being out of work, anyway," he said.

There was a viewing that evening from seven to nine, Grace's mother laid out in a purple dress that had to be taken in four sizes to fit her wasted body. It had been weeks since Grace had seen the old woman wearing her false teeth, and her mouth looked too rigid and severe to be real.

Afterward they stopped at the Anchor Inn Motel and sat downstairs in the nearly empty bar. There was a giant screen on the near wall, a hockey game on with the sound turned down. The players seemed to be moving in slow motion, the game drained of urgency by the silence. Grace wanted a cigarette but was too embarrassed to light up in front of Isaac.

A slender waitress with thickly curled hair to her shoulders brought a tray of drinks to their table and went back to her book behind the bar. Ed thought she was the woman they'd seen recently in a news report, a follow-up story on a national survey in which Newfoundlanders claimed to have sex more frequently than anyone else in Canada. There was a clip of a slender woman with thickly curled hair playing darts in this very bar, saying mainlanders were too uptight to have sex as often as was natural. "Take me, now," she'd said. She pointed the shaft of a dart at the interviewer. She spoke with the intensity of someone who is often disbelieved. "I won't get home tonight till two and I (pause) will still (pause) have sex."

Grace said no, the woman on the news was taller than this one.

Ed took a long drag on his cigarette. "Everyone looks taller on television," he said.

They stayed to the end of the second period and then drove to the old house which had been sitting empty since Grace's mother came to live with her in

St. John's that August. The neighbours had turned on the heat and left lights on for them and put out a Saran-wrapped plate of tea buns and cheese in the kitchen. Grace and Ed went up to bed while Isaac watched the end of the game on the tiny black-and-white set in the living room. Grace could hear its murmur from down-stairs, the sound of skates creasing ice, the rise and fall of crowd noise. She turned to Ed and moved over him, pushing her face into the skin of his neck to muffle the rise and fall of her own voice.

When Grace was a girl her father spent eleven months of the year working at a mine in Black Rock, two days' travel by boat and train from their home in Twillingate. He died in an underground accident when she was seven years old. Her mother never remarried and lived alone in the family home for three decades after Grace left to do her nurses' training at the Salvation Army hospital in St. John's. She had a rotary dial telephone, an oil stove, a black-and-white television that brought in three snowy channels. She grew her own potatoes and cabbage, gave herself insulin injections morning and evening. Never forgot a birthday or anniversary. "Good as a quartz watch," Grace used to say. "She never needs winding."

It was a neighbour of her mother's who called late that summer. She'd noticed that the lights stayed out in the house as it grew dark. When she stepped across the road, she found Grace's mother on the chesterfield where she'd been lying for hours, incoherent and unresponsive. A week later, Grace drove out from St. John's to get her.

The old home always seemed like a doll's house when she came back to it, the ceilings so low Grace could place her palms flat against them, the stairs so narrow a suitcase had to be carried ahead or behind you. She carted her mother's bags awkwardly downstairs, then out to the car. The forecast called for freezing rain in the afternoon and she could feel the threat of it in the wind. When she came back inside she found her mother staring out the single tiny window in the kitchen, the landwash falling away to the grey ocean beyond it.

"We should go," Grace told her.

"Hold on," she said. She was wearing a long grey raglan and black shoes, the strap of her handbag looped over the crook of her elbow. She said, "I'll never look out that window again." There was an odd note in her mother's voice, in the way she said "that window." As if it wasn't her but the window that was about to be taken away from the house for good.

The night Grace met him for the first time, Ed took her to the top of Signal Hill in a cab. The parking lot near the Cabot Tower was empty and black. The stone tower itself was floodlit with stark white light, as if the building was being subjected to some relentless interrogation. There was a low wall around the parking lot that they sat against after the cab dropped them off and they stared out over St. John's. Streetlights terraced the hills above the harbour, clustered rows undulating miles back into the country, a sprawling grid of energy. It was near two in the morning. They could see the cab descending the unlit road below them, tail lights swinging lazily through the winding turns. The red glow flared brighter when the brakes were applied, like someone taking a drag on a cigarette in the dark.

Ed said, "We should have asked him to wait."

Grace looked across at him. He had thinning red hair. His mouth turned down on one side even when he smiled, which gave him an air of tired honesty. She shrugged her shoulders. "I could use the walk," she told him.

Ed nodded and took a pack of cigarettes out of an inside pocket of his coat.

Grace had quit cold turkey when she was thirty-four, the same year she divorced Isaac's father. She had a pack-a-day habit through her marriage, although there was only one cigarette in a dozen that she really enjoyed. Sex with Isaac's father had been much the same, and it had been years since she craved either one.

Ed gave her a wary look when she reached out and helped herself, fishing a cigarette from its neat row. He said, "I didn't see you smoking at the bar."

"It's not a regular thing with me," she told him.

Ed cupped his hands to light her cigarette, then his own. Grace walked across to the opposite side of the parking lot where the hills fell away toward the ocean. She could hear the surf breaking on the headlands and she leaned over the wall as far as she could, staring into the dark as if her eyes might adjust eventually, find enough light to make out shapes in the blackness. She could feel the pulse of the city lights at her back, the nicotine buzz of electricity coursing through thousands of miles of wire and cable. And the dark ocean rolling hundreds of feet beneath her blind stare. It was the beginning of October. She had no idea what she was doing here with this man.

"Maybe we should head home out of it," Ed shouted from across the flat expanse of pavement.

The tests showed her mother's kidneys were deteriorating, a complication related to her diabetes. She went for dialysis three afternoons a week at the Health Sciences Centre, but it was clear there was no hope of recovery, and the sessions left the old woman feeling exhausted and numb. It took two days to get up and around properly afterward. She said it was like being struck by lightning.

"You've been struck by lightning, have you?" Grace said.

Her mother was sitting with her hand over her mouth and nose. She looked away out the living room window. "You know what I mean," she said.

After the third week she refused further treatment, and through that fall her body slowly poisoned itself. She moved about the house with a cane, then with a walker. Eventually she needed help to shower, to go to the bathroom, then simply to feed herself. When the length of the hallway became unmanageable, Grace took a leave of absence from her nursing job. She moved the La-Z-Boy into her mother's room and fed her cups of soup, Jell-O and ice cream, bread soaked in mugs of milky tea.

Her mother began losing her bearings, often living at the old house in Twillingate in her head. At first, there was a childish certainty to her confusion that was almost comical. She mistook Grace for an aunt, for her mother, a friend she hadn't seen since she was a girl. "Where are you now, my love?" Grace would ask her.

"Sure, I'm at Annie's."

"Annie Reid's house, is it? In Crow Head?"

"*Yes,* in Crow Head."

Annie was dead, her house torn down and replaced by a hardware store in the 1950s. Grace laughed to disguise the surge of helplessness that buckled through her. Her mother stared, indignant. Try as she might, she couldn't see the humour in being at Annie Reid's house in Crow Head or understand why she was being teased about it. "Where are *you?*" she'd ask.

Consternation was the word that came to Grace's mind, as she watched her mother struggle, the old woman's childhood crowding in on her mind like weeds choking out a garden. Near the end she was sometimes lucid and lost simultaneously. One afternoon she turned to Grace and said, "You know, Gracie is the only one I got left."

She nodded her head. "Grace told me how much she loves you," she said.

Her mother's room was just large enough for her single bed and the La-Z-Boy chair and the commode Grace signed out on loan from the Red Cross. The air was close with the smell of bedsore linament and the diapers her mother was reduced to wearing and Grace would open the window for the breeze, despite the cold. In heavy weather, when the wind was right, the sound of the foghorn carried up from the shoreline two miles east. If her mother was lucid enough to register it, she made a face and turned her head away. "Oh, my," she'd say. "Close that window, would you?"

"Why, what's wrong with a bit of fresh air?"

"I hates the sound of that foghorn."

Her mother had lived in the lee of that wail all her life, and it made Grace feel suddenly afraid and somehow saddened to learn how much she disliked it. It added to the panic she had begun to feel about herself. For the first time in years she dreaded going to bed alone, lying awake for hours on one side of the mattress, staring into the darkness. Her new loneliness was something with presence and heft, a physical thing chafing at her insides. She was sure it would show up on a chest X-ray like a tumour, a cloudy mass with clearly defined edges.

Grace's friends could see the change in her, but they mistook it for something simpler than it was, for fatigue or sadness. She needed time away from the house, they told her. When she insisted she was fine they nodded their heads quickly and looked down at their shoes, trying to hide their frustration at what they referred to among themselves as Grace's advanced state of denial.

Two of the younger nurses she worked with at Emergency came for her, unannounced, one Friday night. They'd made their own arrangements to have a home care nurse stay with her mother and they stood in the doorway with their coats and shoes on, telling Grace how much better she'd feel if she would only relax for an evening. Grace was surprised at the strength of her reluctance, at the measure of guilt she felt when she walked out to the waiting taxi in a dress and high-heeled shoes. It was unlike anything she'd experienced since she told Isaac she was divorcing his father.

The nurses took her to a small martini bar on Duckworth Street that featured black lights around the baseboards and a relentlessly nebulous soundtrack of acid jazz and trip-hop and house music. Grace had never tried a martini before and couldn't finish her first, the mix of gin and vermouth too unadulterated. She went up to the bar to ask for help picking something else from the elaborate drink menu. Ed wore a dark vest over a white shirt that, in the black light, took on the hue of purple neon. He suggested something called the Stinger. "Good for what ails you," he said brightly.

Grace glanced up at him. Younger than she was, she decided, mid-forties or so. Just past the age when he might be considered good-looking, but not so far that he'd lost the ease that his good looks had conferred. Not predatory, she could see. A cocky, professional flirt. She turned back to the drink list, furious with herself for agreeing to come here. "My mother's dying," she said without looking up. She expected it would shut the man up, wipe the smirk off his face.

He gave her a Stinger on the house. "Lost Mom last year," he told her quietly.

She raised the glass. "Will this help?"

"Briefly," he said. He smiled at her, one side of his mouth turned down. Then he said, "Not much, no."

Grace left with the other nurses an hour and a half later, then came back to the bar alone. She'd had three Stingers by then and ordered another. After Ed closed up they took a cab to Signal Hill and she had her first cigarette in nearly twenty years. She had never slept with a stranger before and she was prepared to be profoundly disappointed. She never expected to hear from him again.

After her divorce, Grace made a conscious effort at self-improvement, as if the failure of her marriage was a sign of some personal shortcoming she could fix by giving up smoking or joining Weight Watchers. She experimented with yoga and transcendental meditation and enrolled in several night courses at the university. She managed to stay off the cigarettes for Isaac's sake, but abandoned the diet after week seven. She'd lost nine and a half pounds, but her nails were chewed to the quick.

As for sociology and psychology, she'd dealt with it all a hundred times on the hospital wards, and there was nothing much new or interesting in any of her courses. She stopped taking notes, preferring instead to doodle aimlessly, or revise a long list of household repairs she couldn't afford. She often forgot which class she was sitting through and, one evening in Anatomy, looked up from her list, surprised to see a diagram of the female genitals on the overhead screen. The professor was in his mid-thirties, with a goatee and a prominent bald spot. He held a metal pointer that extended and retracted like a TV antennae and he was circling a small area of the diagram repeatedly with the plastic tip. Grace had been working as a nurse for fifteen years at the time. She had been married nearly as long.

She went to Isaac's room as soon as she got home. He was in Grade 8 that year and she looked through a stack of books and scribblers until she found the material from his sex education class. She flipped through photocopied essays and questionnaires and diagrams until she found it there. A simple sketch, a line connecting the tiny nub of nerve endings to the unfamiliar italicized word. There was a note beneath it in Isaac's hand-writing: *The clitoris contains twice the number of nerve endings located in the penis.* She sat staring, her arms folded under her breasts, not quite believing her body could have kept such a secret from her. That her thirteen-year-old son could know more about her body than she did herself.

The old house in Twillingate was one of the last on the island to have indoor plumbing installed. When Grace was a girl there was a cast-iron wood stove in the kitchen. One night a week she sat in a wooden tub in front of the fire, and after she went to bed she would hear her mother using the same water: the wet slap of the facecloth, the cupfuls lifted and sluiced across her back.

While her mother was still able to get around that fall, Grace helped her negotiate her way into the tub on Wednesdays and Saturdays. She used the hand-held shower head then while her mother sat on a plastic stool, her arms folded across her stomach like a woman waiting at a bus stop. She was seventy-seven years old. Grace had never before seen her naked.

During the last month of her mother's life, Grace bathed her in her bed, rolling her gently from one side to the other to wash her back and buttocks and legs, her wattled neck and arms, the breasts she had nursed at. The tuft of beautiful silver pubic hair.

Three nights that fall, Grace was convinced her mother was hours from dying, her breath a shallow basin clotted with fluid, one hand flailing helplessly against her chest like a distress signal. She called Ed to come keep her company after his shift at the bar and they sat up together through the small hours of the morning, taking turns at the open window, blowing smoke into the darkness. After sunrise her mother would come to herself, exhausted but remarkably lucid, like a woman who had just endured a difficult labour.

During the first week of November, Grace's mother began asking, "Is it my birthday yet?"

No one had expected she would live this long.

"Ten more sleeps," Grace told her. As if her mother was a child anticipating Christmas. "Eight more sleeps."

By this time Ed was at the house every day, helping Grace lift her mother from her bed to the chair, from the chair to the commode. Her mother took him for another of the nameless home care nurses who came and went. At some point during each visit, he and Grace made love while her mother drifted in and out of sleep in her room. Grace's appetite surprised and embarrassed her. She had never been so greedy for pleasure, and it felt like a betrayal of some kind. But the shame she felt simply made the craving more intense, more compelling.

The day before her mother's birthday, when Grace saw in the old woman's face some sign that she was present and alert, she said, "I've been wanting to tell you, Mom. I've met someone."

The watery blue eyes searched her face.

"I've met a man."

Her mother made a motion with her head, as if acknowledging an acquaintance on the street. "Proper thing," she said.

Grace smiled at her. As far as she knew, her mother hadn't been with anyone after the death of her husband forty years earlier. She didn't know if that was a conscious choice or simply circumstance. She said, "Were you happy, Mom?"

Her mother stared, her eyes shifting quickly back and forth. It was clear she didn't understand what was being asked of her. "I was happy to have you," she said.

The next day Grace and Ed sat on the edge of the bed and sang "Happy Birthday" to her mother in her chair. A cake in the old woman's lap held two candles, 78, each digit topped by a shifting cap of flame. Ed took a picture of Grace kneeling beside her mother to help blow out the candles. She managed to speak lucidly to several people on the phone, asking Isaac about his newborn baby daughter. "She's American, that one," her mother said.

In the weeks following the small birthday celebration, Grace's mother never again got up from her bed. Lying beside Ed in the afternoons, after they'd made love, Grace tried to put herself in her mother's position. She would watch the ceiling and imagine it was the last tiny landscape she would ever look upon. That she would never walk from this room with its mauve walls and chocolate-coloured carpet, or sit up on her own again, or eat a proper meal. She managed to stir up a peculiar sense of claustrophobia in herself, but it felt contrived and weightless, like the fear evoked by a carnival ride.

Ed moved closer to her, waking from a brief sleep, his cock hardening against her thigh as they shifted their bodies toward one another. She reached down to touch him, to feel the pulse and heat of the man centred there. This was real to her. What was happening in the room across the hall was a long, shapeless bad dream she would eventually wake from, even though her mother would not. And in that sense, she knew, it was something the old woman had to suffer alone.

Ed leaned his face into her neck and reached up to wipe the tears from her face with the palm of his hand. "Gracie," he said. "Grace."

"I'm all right," she said. "I'm okay."

She turned to kiss him, the bitter salt taste passed back and forth between them, and she moved slowly down his body to take his cock into her mouth. Ed gathered her hair at the back of her head, holding it tight in his fist while she sucked him, and she felt the sting of it all the way to her toes.

Her mother died just before light, a month to the day after her seventy-eighth birthday. Ed stood at the bedside while Grace weighted the old woman's eyelids with her fingers. "I don't know what she was holding on so long for, poor soul," he said.

Grace brought a pan of warm water to the bedside to wipe her face and neck, to wash the emaciated limbs. She wanted her mother's body to be touched with love one last time before the hearse arrived to collect her.

Ed leaned over her to run his hand through the grey hair, to touch her mother's forehead. "She's so hot," he said, surprised.

Grace opened her mouth but couldn't force a word past the knot galling her throat.

It was the body's internal organs, the heat of them exiting through the skin, dissipating in the cool air of the sick room.

The forecast called for snow the day of the funeral, but all morning a cold, steady drizzle of rain came down. The open water beyond the coves, the low hills of meadow grass and bedrock lost to December fog.

The funeral procession drove up a long dirt road into spruce woods. The hearse passed through rows of headstones toward the back of the cemetery. When her

father was buried here forty years earlier the grave had to
be blasted with dynamite. Along the fence Grace could
see the front-end loader that was used to jackhammer
her mother's grave out of the rock beside her father's
plot.

Ed stood to one side of her, Isaac to the other, holding an umbrella. Those old, hard words from the minister as the casket settled down.

One morning shortly before she died, bedridden,
unable to turn herself or move her legs, unsure who her
daughter was or how old she might be or where she was
lying, her mother had looked at Grace and said, "I'm getting up now the once."

"Yes, my love," Grace said. It was no use to argue,
she knew. They stared at one another a moment longer
and then her mother turned her head toward the wall.

Ed touched Grace's elbow through her coat. The
mourners were moving away from the grave to get in out
of the weather. "We should go, Grace," he said.

The sound of the foghorn pressed in over the trees
and subsided like the tide.

"Grace," he said again.

She nodded her head but didn't move from the spot
where she stood.

"Hold on," she said.

CONTRIBUTORS

Carol Bruneau is the author of two short story collections, *After the Angel Mill* and *Depth Rapture*, and a novel, *Purple for Sky*, which won the Thomas Raddall Atlantic Fiction Award and the Dartmouth Book Award. She lives in Halifax, where she teaches creative writing, and is at work on another novel.

George Elliott Clarke is a revered African–Nova Scotian (Africadian) poet whose prose is as doubtful as his honesty. A Governor General's Award for Poetry (2001) and Portia White Prize (1998) laureate, he is an English professor at the University of Toronto, but, also, a proud landowner in Nova Scotia.

Christy Ann Conlin's first novel, *Heave*, was published in 2002. She was born and raised in Nova Scotia's Annapolis Valley. Her writing has appeared in various literary journals and anthologies. Conlin was the Berwick Fire Prevention Queen when she was fourteen and rode on the fire truck in the Apple Blossom Parade — for her, nothing can rival this experience. She's back in Nova Scotia now.

Kelly Cooper works as an art teacher and makes her home on a dairy farm in Belleisle Creek, New Brunswick. She has been published in literary journals across Canada and was the winner of *The Fiddlehead*'s Fiction Prize and *Grain*'s Short Grain Contest in the spring of 2001. Her work has been included in a number of anthologies and she is one of three writers featured in *Oberon*'s Coming Attractions 2002.

Libby Creelman was born in Cambridge, Massachusetts. She lives with her husband and two children in St. John's, Newfoundland, where she moved twenty years ago. Her short stories have been published in literary magazines across Canada. Her first collection, *Walking in Paradise*, was published by Porcupine's Quill in 2000.

Michael Crummey is a full-time writer living in St. John's. His first novel, *River Thieves*, was nominated for the Giller Prize, the Commonwealth Writers Prize, the Amazon.com/*Books in Canada* First Novel Award, and was awarded the Raddall Atlantic Fiction Prize and the Winterset Award. His latest collection of poetry, *Salvage*, was published by McClelland & Stewart in 2002. A new edition of his book of stories, *Flesh and Blood*, was published by Anchor Canada in 2003.

Larry Lynch is from Miramichi, New Brunswick. His fiction has appeared in various literary journals including *The Fiddlehead*, *The Canadian Forum* and *The Journey Prize Anthology*. His first novel, *An Expectation of Home*, was published by Gaspereau Press in the fall of

2002. Lynch is currently the president of the Writers' Federation of New Brunswick.

Rabindranath Maharaj is the author of two novels, *Homer in Flight*, which was short listed for the Chapters/*Books in Canada* First Novel Award, and *The Lagahoo's Apprentice* — about which the *Toronto Star* wrote, "This may be the best Canadian novel yet written about the Caribbean" — and a collection of short stories, *The Interloper*, which was nominated for the Commonwealth Writers Prize for Best First Book. He was born in Trinidad and now lives in Ajax, Ontario.

Lisa Moore is from St. John's, Newfoundland. She has written two collections of stories: *Degrees of Nakedness*, published by Mercury Press and *Open*, published by House of Anansi. She has written radio, a teeny bit of television, and art criticism. She is a graduate of the Nova Scotia College of Art and Design. She is working on a novel. Moore is the mother of two children.

A graduate of the University of British Columbia's Creative Writing program, Peter Norman has published fiction, poetry, and essays in a variety of Canadian and American periodicals. He is the winner of the 2001 Writers' Union of Canada short prose competition.

Karen Smythe's short stories have appeared in numerous literary journals. Her critical study of Mavis Gallant and Alice Munro, *Figuring Grief: Gallant, Munro and the Poetics of Elegy* (McGill-Queen's University Press), was published in 1992. She has lived in Winnipeg, Toronto,

Regina, and Halifax, and now resides in Sault Ste. Marie, Ontario.

Lee D. Thompson is a native of Moncton, New Brunswick, whose short fiction has appeared in *Gaspereau Review, Nashwaak Review* and *The New Orphic Review*. He has completed a collection of forest stories entitled *In a Dark Wood,* and is now at work on what he is calling an underwater night novel.

R.M. Vaughan was born in Saint John, New Brunswick. His books include the poetry collections *A Selection of Dazzling Scarves* and *Invisible to Predators* (both ECW Press), several poetry chapbooks, the novel *A Quilted Heart* (Insomniac Press), and the play *Camera, Woman* (Coach House Books). Vaughan is the author of fourteen plays, and is the editor of Velvet Touch, an imprint of new Canadian theatre published by Broken Jaw Press. He resides in Toronto, where he is preparing his second novel, *Spells,* for publication with ECW Press in the fall of 2003. He is also at work on a new novel entitled *The Re-Creators.*

Michael Winter is the author of two books that feature Gabriel English: the anthology *One Last Good Look* (contributing stories broadcast on CBC Radio) and the fictional diary *This All Happened* (winner of the inaugural Winterset Award — a prize to which he bears no relation). Both are published by House of Anansi. He loves it when readers assume he writes autobiography, although his family and friends are less pleased. Winter divides his time between Toronto and St. John's.

ACKNOWLEDGEMENTS

There were people I told early on about this project who fortified me immediately with their enthusiasm and support. They were: Denise Bukowski, Maya Mavjee, Christy Ann Conlin, and Charles Barbour.

Rabindranath Maharaj and historian Ian McKay especially deserve singling out for planting the seed.

Thanks to Suzanne Brandreth and Nicholas Massey-Garrison at Doubleday Canada for all the work that made this happen.

Thank you to the contributors to *Victory Meat*, particularly for their patience with my home-office administration skills, but mostly for their generosity and frank talent.

Thank you enormously to everyone who took the time to submit to *Victory Meat*, particularly the talented writers whom I was forced to reject for silly and arbitrary-seeming reasons such as "you're too well established." Many was the time I longed for a co-editor upon whom I could foist responsibility for these often gut-wrenching decisions. Sometimes I considered inventing one.

Atlantic Canada has a wealth of literary history and dogged practitioners who have never left, and have never stopped keeping the faith. I wish to thank and acknowledge these people above all.

LC